T0149418

A STORY UNTOLD

ELYOT RODGERS

BALBOA.
PRESS

A DIVISION OF HAY HOUSE

Balboa Press books may be ordered through booksellers or by contacting:

Balboa Press
A Division of Hay House
1663 Liberty Drive
Bloomington, IN 47403
www.balboapress.com.au
1 (877) 407-4847

Because of the dynamic nature of the Internet, any web addresses or
links contained in this book may have changed since publication and
may no longer be valid. The views expressed in this work are solely those
of the author and do not necessarily reflect the views of the publisher,
and the publisher hereby disclaims any responsibility for them.

The author of this book does not dispense medical advice or prescribe the use
of any technique as a form of treatment for physical, emotional, or medical
problems without the advice of a physician, either directly or indirectly. The
intent of the author is only to offer information of a general nature to help
you in your quest for emotional and spiritual well-being. In the event you use
any of the information in this book for yourself, which is your constitutional
right, the author and the publisher assume no responsibility for your actions.

Any people depicted in stock imagery provided by Getty Images are
models, and such images are being used for illustrative purposes only.
Certain stock imagery © Getty Images.

Print information available on the last page.

ISBN: 978-1-5043-1480-0 (sc)
ISBN: 978-1-5043-1481-7 (e)

Balboa Press rev. date: 05/28/2019

CHAPTER 1

I was sitting in Theo's office within an hour of calling him. I knew of Theo as a very successful businessman involved in real estate. He was identified, somewhat reluctantly, by one of the two private investigators whom I employed to investigate me.

Investigating me was a little unconventional, but it was one of the lessons in life that I had been taught when stepping out of the square, off the so-called calf path, whilst trying to drain the swamp.

After some weeks of not hearing anything from either, I contacted the first investigator. He said, "Mark, you should have received a detailed report by now; I mailed it to you a couple of weeks ago. Yes, you're in a little bit of trouble, and this is covered in my report. If you haven't received it in a couple of days, call me back, and I will send you another copy."

"What sort of trouble?" I asked.

"It's all in the report. I won't talk about it on the phone. Call me back in a couple of days if you haven't received it."

I never received his report.

I waited a week before I tried to call Evan back on several occasions, only to find that he was unavailable on the phone. For a variety of reasons, he would not talk to me. Eventually, his wife came to the phone and indicated that they were too busy to do anything for me. I would not be getting a bill. "Do not call back," she said.

Based on the previous conversation I had had with Evan a few days earlier, I was confused, but trying to contact him was futile—and now he would not even talk to me.

I called the second investigator. "Hello, Colin. This is Mark. I asked you to do some work for me a few weeks ago, and as I haven't heard from you, I thought I would give you a call to check on your progress."

"Mark, I have been advised to not do anything for you. You're interfering in someone's business activities, and they want you to stop."

Somewhat taken aback, I attempted to use the wise men, going down the who, what, why, where, when, and how track. "Colin, whose business am I interfering with, and how?"

"I am not allowed to tell you," he replied.

"That's crazy. How am I supposed to stop doing what I have been doing that is causing a problem, without knowing what I am doing to whom?"

"You're in deep, Mark. I can't do anything for you. In fact, I have been told to stay away from you. I have been warned off."

"Look. If you don't tell me what I am doing, how am I supposed to end this situation?"

"I have been told to leave it alone and not do or say anything more to you. I can do no more for you."

I could still not work out what I was doing to bring about this situation. For some time, we were just going around in circles. Colin would not reveal anything apart from telling me that I was in very deep and he would not, could not, do any more for me. He repeated, "I have been told to stay away from you."

"Look," I repeated, getting increasingly frustrated, "how am I supposed to know whose business I am interfering with, and how, unless you tell me or give me the name of the person who warned you off? Maybe I could go see him and find out more."

"There's no point," said Colin. "He won't see you."

"That's my problem," I said.

Eventually, he gave me Theo's name. I was surprised. From what I knew, Theo had made his money in real estate and was regarded as a very successful businessman. What on earth was I doing that would affect Theo?

Only half believing what I had been told, I hopped onto a plane the next day and booked into a hotel on the esplanade, a few hundred yards from where I used to live.

I loved the beachside suburbs and used to spend a lot of time walking or lazing there.

The next morning, I rang Theo. I got straight through. I told him who I was and that I wanted to see him. "What about?" he asked.

"Well, I have been told by a couple of private investigators I hired that I have been interfering in your business. They advised me that they had been told *by you* to not do any work for me."

"Where are you? Can you be here in an hour?"

"Yes," I said.

The tram terminus was within one hundred metres from where I was staying. I had a quick shave and shower, and within half an hour of that call, I was sitting in a tram on my way to meet Theo.

On arrival, I was ushered into Theo's office. It was large and tastefully furnished. Theo's desk was in keeping with his surroundings—very much of the older wooden style.

I introduced myself, and at the same time, I looked in one corner at another man who appeared to be a younger version of Theo. He hovered there for several minutes without introducing himself, coming closer, or conducting any of the normal pleasantries. He was totally ignoring me.

Finally, he looked at Theo and then left. I guessed him to be Theo's son, there in case my behaviour became unruly.

Theo was of average height, a little overweight, balding, and obviously of European descent. For some time, Theo and I exchanged pleasantries.

"Theo, I have been told that I have been interfering in your business, and the reason I have asked to see you is to determine what I am doing that is affecting you. Where are you from? What are you, a Greek or Italian boy?"

"No."

"Are you married?"

"Not now."

"Do you live locally?"

"No. I now live interstate. I used to live locally, but after my divorce, I went interstate. So, what do you want to see me about?"

"Well, I engaged a couple of investigators to investigate me, but later they told me they could not help me because they had been warned by you not to do anything for me because I was interfering in your business. I could not see how, and they could not tell me what I was doing that was affecting you. I thought I would come and talk to you about it."

Theo initially appeared to take no notice of what I was saying and continued with a host of questions.

"You used to live locally?

"Yes. I went to live interstate after my wife and I divorced."

"Can't you reconcile with your wife?"

"No, it's beyond that. We are now divorced."

The pleasantries went on for what seemed an eternity, but it was about twenty minutes. We talked about many things, but not what I had come to talk about. Theo's manner was friendly and congenial. I was beginning to think of him as a delightful person. *The investigators must have got it all wrong,* I thought.

Suddenly, as if a tap had been turned on, Theo's whole demeanour changed from affable to aggressive, leaving me astounded.

"Look. Let me give you some fatherly advice," he said. "Yes, we know who you are. You have been interfering in something you know nothing about. Stop it now. Do not go onto the television again. Do not continue to do what you've been doing. Yes, we've been watching you, and we will continue to do so. You are still in contact with your friends here, talking to the press and going on radio and television. Stop it. If they contact you, tell them you had a mental lapse and you've since got over it."

Stunned, I asked, "How does my appearing on television to bring about greater equality for the noncustodial parent, as well as my attempting to obtain equality in divorce, going to affect you and your business?" This was the only reason I had been on radio and TV.

Somewhat angrily, Theo answered, "I won't tell you again. You are interfering in something you know nothing about. Leave it alone. You are already a marked man in New York, and if you continue, you will be found in the back of a burned-out car. Go away. Don't talk to the press, your friends, or anyone, and it will settle down. You'll be watched to make sure you're taking my advice. Do you understand?"

"Yes. I don't know what this is about, but I will stop."

Somewhat stunned, I really could not remember any more of what I said. But it must have been the right answer because Theo reverted to his affable self whilst escorting me out of his office.

While I sat in the tram on the way back to the motel, Theo's words, together with the vehemence with which they were delivered, kept ringing in my ears. To say I was on an emotional roller coaster would be an understatement. I had trouble understanding. I was filled with fear, anger, doubt—a complete mix of emotions. Could it really have happened? I had just sat through the meeting, so I knew it had. I wasn't delusional—something I had been wondering about for a while now.

What in the world was going on? How could I, by starting an organisation to bring about greater equality for a noncustodial parent in a divorce situation, have brought this on? How could I have interfered with someone who owned large buildings and other real estate? How could

Theo be affected by what I was doing? I was interfering with something I knew nothing about. Somehow, I was interfering with Theo's business.

I had started a group for non-custodial parents, primarily fathers, to equalise what I thought was an unfair situation. In most cases, custody is generally awarded to the mother, with the father being granted access and relegated to the position of being, as I called it, a father once a fortnight. To me, this situation as it was established, and the mechanism used within the system, was not in the best interests of the children or the father. It appeared to be strongly in favour the mother.

Initially, when I separated from my wife, the split was quite amicable. I would see my daughters quite frequently, almost weekly. I continued to do maintenance around what was the marital home and have access to my two daughters as often as I required. My ex-wife and I had worked out some very amicable arrangements on both the use of our home as security for my business and access to my two daughters.

The learning curve of a separation was about a ninety-degrees climb with a variety of mixed emotions. I remembered when I used to go back to my unit, after seeing the girls each week and spending time with them at the house where I used to live. After the visits, when I got home, I would go straight into the shower, sobbing uncontrollably until I could regain my composure.

This situation changed drastically when my ex-wife started divorce proceedings. I could now only have access to my daughters at predetermined times, every alternate weekend. I could no longer spend time doing things at the house with and for the girls. I was to pick them up only at predetermined times, and spending time working on the house was no longer an option.

I was no longer allowed to use our house as security for my business. I only became aware of this when my assistant came back from the bank one Friday to tell me, "The bank manager asked me to get you to call him. He would not cash the payroll cheque."

"Why not? Did he say?"

"No, he just said to call him."

I immediately called the bank manager to ask what in the hell was going on.

"Mark, I have been instructed by head office to freeze your account because the security you posted has been withdrawn by your wife's solicitor. I can let today's paycheque go through, but you had better make alternative arrangements for next week."

Based on that, I immediately rang my ex-wife. "What is going on? My bank account has been frozen. I cannot draw the money to pay the staff, and the bank manager tells me that the direction came to him from the head office, on the instructions from your solicitor. Did you cause this?"

"No. My solicitor has told me I was not to let you use the house as security, so I presume that he has advised the bank."

"You know what effect this is going to have on my business? If I cannot use the house, I cannot continue with the business. You know that, don't you? Why are you doing this?"

"I am following the instructions of my solicitors. If I don't do what they tell me, they will not represent me."

Somewhat disgusted I put down the phone. This episode started the end of my business and my supply line.

Shortly afterwards, I was told by my solicitor that I was not allowed to go near the children's school or their after-school care facility; people feared that I may run away with them. When I asked, this too was blamed on advice from the solicitors. "Can they do this?" I asked.

"Yes, if it is deemed appropriate."

The flexibility that I and my ex-wife had shared with custody was now restricted to my fortnightly visits. On occasions, these visits were not allowed because the children were "not available".

Further, arrangements were made by my wife for calisthenics for the girls every Saturday morning and church attendance every Sunday morning. As a result, I saw my girls on two half days each fortnight.

This was also sometimes changed because the girls had to be somewhere or were staying at a friend's house. When I asked my ex-wife as to why these changes had come about, the reply was that she was acting under her solicitor's instructions. This situation continued for months as the restrictions built up. Always the question remained: was it the solicitors or my ex-wife using the girls as a weapon? Fighting it involved more court appearances, with the resulting escalating fees.

I can remember on more than one occasion that I would turn up to pick up my daughters on my custodial weekend, knock on the front door of the house, and be confronted by my ex-wife, who said, "You cannot have the girls this weekend. They wanted to stay at their friend's house overnight, so I let them."

"Well, can I have them next weekend instead?"

"No. I have arranged to take them away."

On one instance when I went to pick up some material that I had left in the house, my ex-wife would not let me in. This caused me to call the police, only to be advised that they could do nothing. I had to go back to the solicitors and the courts on Monday. This incurred more legal costs by way of solicitors, court fees, and spiralling expenses, further destroying my deteriorating financial position.

Situations of this type increased, and this appeared to be intentional, but by whom? My ex-wife, or the solicitors?

During this stage, I was so embroiled in my situation that it would be fair to say clear thinking was not an attribute I enjoyed. Increasingly, a degree of animosity developed.

One afternoon, whilst having a cup of coffee with a friend and work associate of mine, we compared notes. Tony and I used to work for the same computer company involved in scientific computing; I was the branch manager locally, and Tony was on things technical, interstate. We had developed quite a friendship over time, and this developed further when Tony transferred locally with another company.

Tony was also going through a separation process with his ex-wife. It was during these discussions that we noticed many common denominators.

Access to our children was being frustrated. Property settlement and other common aspects became an issue. It appeared that an adversarial situation between the husband and wife was established and fostered in both cases. It was then that Tony and I agreed things were quite amicable prior to the divorce process starting. As Tony said, "Mate, the bills just keep coming in. In and out of court appearances, conferences called between our solicitors and my ex and me. I just want a degree of normalcy back into the situation. Costs are being escalated dramatically, and a hell of a lot of time is being taken going over things that have been put to bed already by my wife and me. This is also creating tension between my wife and I, and it's fast turning into a hostile situation. When I ask her what is going on, she tells me that she is following her solicitor's instructions."

I could only agree. My situation was being made more tenuous daily because I was unable to work my business. My capital reserves were being depleted. It appeared that both Tony and I were experiencing the same situational factors.

Our sentiments were that the solicitors were a bunch of bastards generating an income stream of millions from people who could not afford it and were having enough trouble with their lives without someone adding to the situation.

Because of our meeting, Tony and I decided to place an advertisement in the daily papers requesting non-custodial parents or fathers in a similar situation to contact us. We set up a meeting at Doug's house, another friend going through a divorce, and invited some of the people to attend.

During the meeting, we talked to primarily fathers separated and going through the process. During the meeting, we established a heavy number of common denominators within the system that we had all been experiencing.

This caused us to place a few more advertisements within the daily papers to promote the organisation, and as a result, we received calls from fathers locally and interstate, as well as from daily newspapers. I was then contacted by one of the local television stations in relation to the current divorce situation and asked to appear on the afternoon current affair television shows.

During this initial interview, I was asked by Ray, "What are you trying to achieve?"

I answered, "A better situation for all concerned. The present method is unfair towards the non-custodial parent and certainly is not in the best interest of the children.

"In which way?" Ray asked.

"Well, adversarial situation established between the parents within the current divorce processes, with a number of accusations that are often untrue. Accusations of child molestation, interference, and cruelty are just some of them. I have been accused of being a communist and interfering with my daughter, and now I am branded. There will always be a percentage of people who will believe this. To some, all my protestations and denials will be wasted. We have established that this too is part of the methodology in the system. Because of this, I believe that perhaps we should look at alternative ways of achieving a more positive result."

"How do you see this happening?" Ray asked.

"Well, one such option would be to establish a number of five- or seven-person panels to hear matters in relation to a divorce, and to work with the parents to develop a more amicable solution."

This was taken up by the local press, who then conducted a series of interviews with me, a child psychologist, and other people involved in this situation. The psychologists tended to agree with me and implied that in their experience, they had witnessed and voiced their dismay at the results of the current system—and more important, at the long-term effects on the children.

My suggestion of a panel was ridiculed by a senior executive from the law society, and as a result, all I really achieved was to incur the wrath of the legal profession, including my own solicitor. I had my fifteen minutes of fame and a further onrush of what I called the funnies.

It was shortly after this I elected to leave and go interstate to start a new life. All the time, I asked was this trigger for the funnies, or did it simply add to it? Or was this standard fare in a divorce process?

I went back to the hotel; it was right on the esplanade overlooking the beach and somewhat older in style, but it suited me perfectly. I changed and sat on the beach, right across from where I used to live.

It was a beautiful sandy beach with the customary buildings. Behind this was a grass strip separating the beach from the road.

It was a sunny autumn day with few people around. I could always sit quietly, listen to the surf, and reflect on the happenings in my life, returning a degree of peace, tranquillity, and sanity.

Listening to the surf was somewhat a misnomer. The place was situated in the gulf, and although it was a seaside suburb, surf was not an attribute it could boast in keeping with a lot of the other suburban beaches of its type. It was more the gentle lapping of the water. But I loved these beaches for what they were. The water was clean, and having lived in a nearby suburb for many years, and given where I lived was just a five-iron shot from the beach, I remembered walking and being on the beach with my daughters.

I remembered the times that I used to spend, being at a loss and not knowing to what to do with my daughters. I talked to other fathers in the same situation to get ideas. I experienced the somewhat surreal situation of taking them to a park to play on the swings, or the zoo or the beach, and the other things one can do on two afternoons each fortnight.

I was distressed when I left Theo's office. I experienced a range of emotions that were frightening and confusing. But through the anguish and distress came some positive factor that I became aware of only after sitting and reflecting for some time. Theo had stated quite clearly that yes, he knew me and that "we" had been watching me for some time. Further, "we" would continue to do so. He told me to leave "it" alone, whatever the hell it was. I really had no idea.

Finally, I had some explanation for some of the funnies I had been experiencing initially when I was living locally, and later when I moved interstate.

Was it when my wife started divorce proceedings, or when I started the Children of Divorce group?

Clearly my flat had been entered on more than one occasion in my absence. Initially I lived alone in a two bedroom unit, one room for me and one for my daughters on days of custody. The unit had been organised by my and my ex-wife's mutual friend.

When I came home from work, I would often smell somebody's body odour in my unit. Whoever he was, personal hygiene was not an issue he had considered. This was just one of the elements that prompted me to think that maybe I was delusional.

On another occasion, I had put some old clothes in a collection bag from one of the charities that had been left on my doorstep. This included some worn underpants that had been given to me by a friend after she realised that I was wearing Y-fronts. This had caused her to break up laughing at the time. Julie had taken one look at my underpants, grabbed my total stock from the cupboard, and threw them in the bin outside. "Promise me that you will not retrieve them. Stay here whilst I go out and get you something more appropriate." She then went out and bought what she deemed to be more in keeping. Y-fronts were not an option.

I smiled as I remembered those silly moments amidst my feeling that this batch had passed their "use by" date and were now ready for retirement.

One morning several weeks later, whilst getting ready for my shower, I went into the cupboard to retrieve some clean underwear. To my surprise, the underwear that I had put out for collection some weeks ago was now on top of my clean underwear pile in the cupboard.

I was shocked because I knew I had thrown them out some weeks ago. This caused another consultation with some of the wise men: what, how, why, who? Confusion reigned!

In another instance, the clock in my car had stopped working, stuck on the same time for months. this had initially happened about two years previously, and as other priorities preceded the clock, it did not cause me any concern. I did not seek to have it rectified.

One weekend I decided that mine was now a tired little Peugeot that had served me well and had managed to survive the many onslaughts that had been bestowed on it, both locally and interstate.

Retirement from these constant incidences were in order, and so I went to a couple of motor dealers to check about trading it in, buying a new one, and any alternatives.

On Monday as I went to start the car on the way to the office, I glanced at the clock. To my surprise, not only was the clock working, but it was within a couple of minutes of the radio time. As they say, "That's funny. How did that happen?"

This was another inexplicable event that plagued me at that time, leaving me confused and unsettled. How did a clock in a car stop working for about two years, and then overnight inexplicably start and adjust itself to the correct time on the day after I went to motor dealers to see about a trade-in?

Once more I pondered the wonders of modern science and the possibilities as to how this could happen. It was parked overnight on the street because this was its usual resting place.

While sitting at the beach, I reflected on this situation and the funnies going on in my life. Some of these events had acted as the trigger for me to go interstate. I wanted to clear the clouds that got in the way.

CHAPTER 2

woke up to a cold, wet July morning. The wind cut through every opening it could find as I pulled the covers to stay cosy, listening to the rain pounding on the windows outside. I lay there for a few minutes thinking about my situation. I looked at my watch: it was a little after five. I had plenty of time, so I lay there listening to the wind howling outside, increasing and decreasing in intensity.

After a few minutes, I quietly slipped out of bed, put on my tracksuit, went into the kitchen, made a cup of tea, and settled myself into the in the lounge room. It was still dark outside; the rain beat against the windows. Despite this, inside was very peaceful, quiet, and cosy.

I sat down and took a gulp of my tea, enjoying the quiet, peaceful warmth.

Sometime later, Terri came out to cook breakfast. She had obviously been, crying which made me feel bad.

I had met Terri several months ago at a club in town. I was still going through the funnies after my divorce, and so I took it very easy when it came to letting any relationships develop. But Terri had broken down some of the barriers and increasingly become a part of my life.

Terri was almost a teacher; with about twelve months to go before she was qualified. She too had been through a divorce and had a couple of young boys. To make ends meet, she used to work in the kitchen at the hotel across the road as a kitchen hand. This gave her some extra money whilst in college.

The relationship with Terri started very slowly, and I would only see her once every two to three weeks. We eventually saw more and more of each other, often spending the night at each other's house.

It was during this period that John offered me a job interstate and the potential to re-establish my supply line. I had been forced to close my business and was in the throes of looking for employment. The requirement of eight hundred dollars in monthly maintenance, which I had no way of paying, did not help my situation.

I did not want to leave Terri on a note like this—me travelling interstate to start a new life and at the same time leaving a growing relationship with Terri. As result, we did not say much as we ate breakfast, and I avoided the subject of leaving. It had all been said a million times before.

"Look, John has a job for me. It isn't much, but I could re-establish the supply line that, as you know, has been cut. When I am established, maybe you and the boys can come over, and we can set up interstate."

"Why can't you get a job locally and stay here?"

"Don't you think I have been trying? But so far, it's no-go. I'm just not getting anywhere. Besides, maybe if I go interstate, things will settle down and the interference will stop."

I attributed a large part of this situation to the stress of the divorce, the constant battle with my wife's solicitors, and the combination of strange happenings in my unit and in all areas of my life.

All of this contributed to my feelings of self-doubt, uselessness, and paranoia. Maybe some sort of sanity would return to my life with the job. Money would be coming in again. I could make a fresh start and re-establish myself.

I finished my breakfast, my reminiscing, and all the other things I had used to defer leaving. It was finally time to get into the car and drive.

I planned to make it to make it a two-day trip and cruise into my hometown the next day. It was a good day for driving: cold, wet, and windy. This did nothing to help my mood or disposition at all as I finished my coffee and made all the necessary noises about going.

Terri came out with me as I got into the car. We had said our goodbyes many times before, and so we kept it short when I left. Terri was trying unsuccessfully to not cry, and I felt low for a variety of reasons.

Leaving a growing relationship with Terri was not sitting well with me at all. I had not seen my daughters for several months and felt guilty every day, when I thought about them.

I wanted to fight back, but I could not pin down whom to fight. My ex-wife was obviously guilty of something, but just how much and what, I could not determine with any degree of certainty.

Her words kept ringing in my ears: "I will destroy you physically, financially, and psychologically. I'll see you digging ditches before I am through with you."

My solicitor had warned me that I had the temerity to leave her not once but twice, and she would seek revenge. My solicitor was a female, and so I believed that she was ordained to speak on things female, at least more than I was.

I had long since established that my knowledge of things female was scant. This was not helped when doing a managerial psych course in my younger days. The instructor started a lecture on understanding women by putting a blank slide on the overhead and promptly telling us that was how much he understood, thereby wishing us well with the tasks involved with women. This was my initial insight into a complex subject.

With hindsight, it would have been safer, less painful, and eventually less expensive if I had declared myself insane, given my wife everything, and gone bush. But I felt I was made of sterner stuff and would fight the good fight.

This attitude was fostered when I gave up accounting, first started in sales, and was given some material that I kept. Some of the words kept coming back to me when I hit a low point.

> When you're lost in the wild, and you're
> scared as a child,
> And death looks you bang in the eye.
> And your sore as a boil, it's according to Hoyle
> To cock your revolver and die.

But the code of a man, says, "Fight all you can,"
And self-dissolution is barred.
In hunger and woe, oh, it's easy to blow …
It's the hell-served-for-breakfast that's hard.

You're sick of the game! Well, now, that's a shame.
You're young and you're brave and you're bright.
You're had a raw deal! I know-but don't squeal.
Buck up do your damndest and fight.

It's the plugging away that will win you the day,
So, do not be a piker, old pard!
Just draw on your grit; it's so easy to quit:
It's the keeping-your-chin-up that's hard.

—Ted Tiltins

I regarded myself as being in a very serious situation. I lived through it for some time in a daze, switching between realities: what I thought was paranoia, total insanity, and all things in between.

Now I was leaving to live interstate, destroyed financially, in many ways psychologically scarred, and frustrated with a feeling of defeat. I felt like I had cornered the market on feeling bad and had turned it into an art form. I considered myself relatively intelligent and wondered how I'd let myself get into this situation.

It was at times like these that I resorted to "When You're Lost in the Wild".

I was at a total loss, trying to understand the situation and circumstances surrounding me, but I had lived through the funnies, so belief and uncertainty were always governing factors. Some of the elements of good, old-fashioned fear, uncertainty, and doubt had crept in.

Somewhere in the back of my mind, I always came back to, "Hey, you saw it, felt it, and touched many of the happenings. You smelt many body odours in the unit when you came home after being out either socialising or at work. You have had to pay money for expenses incurred for you. You saw, smelt, and touched things that had been changed in your absence. So, think about it and get real."

These, as well as the rigors of the divorce, combined to make me think that maybe a new start interstate might alleviate the situation and diffuse the animosity that now existed between my ex-wife and I. If I started a new life, maybe it would also stop the funnies.

The situation between my wife and I had gone from something amicable to one of pure hostility and frustration. It was many years before I could establish that this was a contrived situation.

I was not alone. Thousands of people go through a marriage break-up. But at this stage, I directed my animosity towards the solicitors. They were a bunch of bastards, strutting around and dictating and construing the ensuing activities.

My belief was that either my ex-wife or the solicitors (or both) had engineered this objective. This outcome was engineered by them. Little did I know at that time about my increasing exposure to the learning curve.

CHAPTER 3

While heading north and not far from the city by-pass, I found myself behind a semi that was throwing a mixture of oil, slush, and mud onto the windscreen. Being so close to the bypass, I decided to wait behind until it was safer. I slowed down and put some distance between myself and the semi. As I did, I noticed that a warning light on the dashboard was flashing, indicating that my brake pads needed replacing. I had just picked up my car from the crash repairer, and this was one of the jobs on the list, so I dismissed the light as a loose connection. This thought was assisted by the fact that the brakes were working very well, whereas before they had been a little dodgy and squeaky.

Although I blessed the Peugeot people for letting me know when my brakes needed attention, I cursed the mechanic for not doing the job properly and leaving me with the nagging doubt that maybe they had not done it. The brakes had worked perfectly since I'd picked up the car, and so I put the light down to a loose connection.

Some weeks previously whilst attending a businessmen's breakfast, I parked my car on the street about a hundred metres from the motel where the meeting was to be held. After the meeting, when I returned to my car, I discovered that someone had run into it. The damage to the car was quite extensive and could not be driven.

Nobody claimed responsibility, and as a result, I was without transport, further out of pocket, and now at the stage when I was being lent money to live on by friends. This was another episode that caused me to wonder what was going on. Was I being harassed? For what purpose, and by whom?

There were inexplicable malfunctions and happenings in my flat, together with the malfunctions I had experienced in every facet of my life. Much later, I remembered what I called the Hertzberg factor, which came into effect and in many ways had become the standard method of operation. "Give them heaps, and when they complain, accuse them of paranoia." The writings according to Hertzberg were something I'd had exposure to during training.

There were many episodes of obstruction from what I thought was my ex-wife in relation to seeing my daughters on my fortnightly weekend access rights. One was that I was mentally unstable, and she was afraid as to what I might do.

I was forced to go back to the psychiatrist not long after when my wife tried to stop me from seeing the girls, indicating that she was afraid for their safety because I had been inside a mental institution.

"What are you doing? Why have you tried to say that I was mentally unstable?"

"Well, you are in a private hospital under the care of a psychiatrist."

"Yes, you are right, I am. I stay there at night and go about my business each day. I come and go as I please. He did not want me living alone now."

To offset this, I had to obtain a referral from my doctor to the psychiatrist. The first thing I discovered early was that I sat on a chair and was not required to lie on a couch. This was a little disappointing because the chair had a wooden seat, which became quite hard after a period.

After a few hours, a few visits, and several hundred dollars, the psychiatrist said, "Mark, if you are nuts, then everybody else is as well. You are no worse than any of them."

This offered me some consolation, but now the funnies became a greater source of puzzlement and confusion and when the concepts of Twiggies training, Christianity, and "When You're Lost in the Wild" kicked in.

Three visits and a few hundred dollars poorer, I had to go back to the court, where my wife's solicitor stood up and accused me of being mentally unstable and being admitted to a mental hospital, adding that I was under the care of a psychiatrist responsible for my admittance.

My solicitor disputed this and told him about the letter from my psychiatrist. The judge then turned to me and asked, "What is the situation? Why are you seeing a psychiatrist?"

"Your Honour, I sought a referral from my doctor, initially to try to make some things clearer in my own mind. There is a lot going on with my divorce, which is turning out to be messy with a high degree of aggression. I am merely trying to sort out fact from fiction. I have not been inside a mental hospital, and I have a letter from my psychiatrist confirming that, as well as confirming that I am not mentally unstable. He put me in a private hospital to give me a break from what was going on around me at the time."

"Do you have the letter with you?" asked the judge.

"Yes, Your Honour," I replied. I gave the letter to the judge.

The judge took one look at the letter and ruled in my favour. I won access rights on the strength of the letter explaining that I was sane and of sound mind. The shrink suggested that he was seeing the wrong party and should be seeing my ex-wife.

This was good, but I was another two and a half thousand dollars poorer, plus the cost of the shrink. That totalled over three thousand dollars for another episode of separation stupidity.

My leaving to go interstate under the circumstances brought about a strong bout of depression. I was leaving my girls after having not seen them for a while, and I had feelings of guilt for having abandoned them. Much of this situation was brought about by my activity or lack thereof. How much was caused by indirect action by my wife and her solicitors? How did her solicitors know that I was seeing a psychiatrist and had been in a private hospital? I never broadcasted it.

I was leaving a growing relationship with Terri and my friends. This caused me to feel that driving in front of the semi and braking hard on the wet road might be a good idea. But as Frankie says, "My heart just won't buy it." Together with the thought that self-dissolution is barred, that caused me to slip Dvorak's *New World* into the cassette player and listen to the music.

This used to be my ex-wife's favourite piece, and it had become one of mine. I found the melody quite haunting, and as always, I was carried by the music. The combination of my thoughts and Dvorak did not help my feeling of total hopelessness and helplessness, which acted as the trigger for the waterworks to start. Feelings of total frustration and defeat caused me to scold myself for allowing my emotions to come to the front and let my weakness show.

CHAPTER 4

The weather cleared progressively, and the rain stopped. In the distance, the sky was starting to clear, and large patches of blue sky emerged. In fact, it was now bright and sunny. The blue skies and sunny outlook transferred to my feelings, making me feel not so gloomy and despondent. I sat back and enjoyed the drive while I let my mind drift back to some of the events that had taken place.

My thoughts made sense, but I did not know where to start to prove whether I was right or wrong on some of it or all of it I started by trying to reconstruct in chronological order some of the incidents that I had experienced.

Embracing the ideas that the divorce situation is a well-constructed system and establishing and building aggression and an adversarial position between the two parties, is but part of it.

I followed the train of thought whilst driving the next day, and I appreciated the opportunity to give something my complete and undivided attention—something I had not had the opportunity to do for several months. I was glad when I eventually got to my destination at about four in the afternoon. I really appreciated the opportunity to think things through, go over a lot of what had transpired, and start assembling the sequence that the events had taken place.

Some of these events included my regularly finding that the seat position of my car had been altered from where I had left it the night before. This was in relation to the incline as well as the positioning from the steering wheel. Further, after I switched off the motor, a noise that sounded like a tape rewinding came from behind the dashboard. It could not be explained by any mechanic that I spoke to and to date remained a mystery.

On one of the many times I was experiencing car troubles, I noticed that the accelerator pedal was sticking. The mechanic told me that my automatic transmission needed to be overhauled. After the overhaul at a cost of seven hundred dollars, I found that nothing had changed, and then it turned out to be the accelerator cable that was frayed. I was always asking myself whether this revenue-generating situation from my mechanic was a genuine mistake, another way of increasing my costs, or something more. I never really knew.

My car being interfered with paired with many other unsettling events happening in my life, the least of which were expenses incurred for me at a rate of knots. I initially put it down to my ex-wife and the private investigators obtaining leverage and evidence for the divorce, but it had continued after the divorce proceeding were completed, which was puzzling. Often this left me feeling that perhaps I was mistaken and was reading more into things that were not right. The self-doubt started. I doubted what I saw, believed, and in some cases witnessed, often wondering if the strain of the break-up was too much for me and if I was in the advanced stages of paranoia, ready for the funny farm.

Now, after all this time, I had established that there was something more, but I was having incredible difficulty getting any form of connectivity between my divorce situation, my publicly voicing my feelings for the children of divorce and the methodology or system used to achieve a divorce, and Theo.

I had gone through a divorce. So what? It was happening increasingly every day. Anyone would say that it in many ways, it was a cleansing process. When the solicitors said, "Let's get this settled so that you can get over this and rebuild your life. Put this behind you and start again," this seemed to me to be a sound proposition.

At that time, I really was in a state of turmoil. Psychologically, I questioned my own sanity. Financially, I wondered at my ability to survive, and I questioned how this would be achieved. The thought of a modicum of peace returning and starting a new life appeared to be the ideal avenue. In fact, after all the rigors of the situation I had been living through for the last few years, settlement and getting it finished was a blessed relief.

The next morning, feeling fresh after a good sleep, I thought I would quickly climb under the car to replace the loose wire that was causing the indicator light to flash intermittently. Sure enough, it was a wire hanging loose on the inside of the front driver's side wheel, and about two inches away was the male fitting. It took me all of two seconds to slide the female fitting with the wire attachment into the male wheel attachment, and in a moment the job was done.

As I started sliding out from under the car, my eye caught something on the tyre, and so I moved over to have a closer look. As I did, I went cold. I felt physically sick in the stomach and as scared as a child.

The inside of the tyre had a neat cut from just short of the tread to the rim. I could see the canvas. Yesterday and the day before, I was approaching speeds of up to 140 kilometres per hour whilst driving across the plains. If that tyre had blown at that speed, I would not have had a ghost of a chance. I would have lost control and gone into oncoming traffic, probably rolling the car. I shuddered and thanked the man with the sandals, shepherds crook, long gown, and bearded.

The tyre had obviously been deliberately cut; it was too clean and straight to be anything else Whatever had been used to cut it had to be sharp and strong to get through the layers the way it had. It was no accident that it had happened. This was confirmed when I took the car to have the tyre changed.

When the mechanic saw it, his opening words were, "Mate, someone must be trying to get rid of you. This cut is no accident. To get through the layers of canvas that they have, they would have had to cut through with a sharp knife because they have gone through several layers. You're a lucky man, or someone must be looking after you. You say that you had just come across from the plains with a tyre like that? It could have blown at any minute."

"Thank you. You are positive it was cut and not an accident, not a by-product of the accident when someone ran into it when it was parked?"

"No, that is a definite cut. That is no accident. You must have upset someone somewhere."

I felt stunned disbelief.

This event took place before the proliferation of mobile phones and cameras. Further, I did not save the tyre, photograph it, or keep any evidence, and so later I simply had my explanation of events.

Based on the tyre being cut, which I saw—as did the mechanic who replaced it—I had to accept that it happened. If I accepted that, then I must accept that someone wanted me to have an accident. Did they know that I was going to be travelling interstate across the plains? How? Although I had not kept it a secret, I did not broadcast it. And who in the hell were *they*, anyway? This was a definite attempt to cause me to have an accident.

I had a lot of difficulty accepting this and accepting that someone was trying to kill me. I did not know who or why. Again, good old-fashioned FUD came back into play—fear, uncertainty, and doubt. Possibly it was my ex-wife, but this was stupid. It could have been the same people who had organized the entering and funnies in my flat. Why, and to what purpose?

Maybe I was right about the thoughts I had in the car, and they thought I knew too much and could damage their operation. If they could do this, what would they do next? I did not know. I only knew I was frightened. What did they think I knew? In fact, what *did* I know? What was I perceived to be in danger of exposing? I really had no idea. More clouds covered my horizons.

Like any of us in this circumstance, my mind took over. Right brain, left brain, logic, and emotion become strange companions. My thinking could not be classed as being totally rational at times; cognitive bolstering ran rampant.

This was done in a manner so that it would look like an accident. "Must do" took over from "like to do", and I again cast my thoughts to who, what, and why.

I went back over the events to see if I could get some calm into the situation, only partially accepting that I had a problem and should address it. I still did not really accept that I had a problem.

Step one was to clearly identify just what the problem was. To me, a fundamental problem was that someone was trying to kill me. But really, was this the problem or a symptom?

Perhaps my spreading rumours about having written and recorded information with several people that would come to light in the event of something happening to me was the trigger for the accidental death appearance of the tyre incident.

Was my getting on television and talking about an alternative to the current methodology a causative factor? Was this the trigger for the harassment? How much was real, and how much imagined and triggered by fear, fact, fantasy, or fiction was never clear at any stage and always appeared to merge.

Talking to people was a waste of time and an exercise in futility, with the only result being that I did an excellent job convincing people that I was totally around the twist, heavy with symptoms of paranoia; so. From that point on, I thought. *Shut up, soak it up, and keep your thoughts to yourself.*

With all the thoughts that had been swimming around for the last two days while going over the happenings of the last several months, my emotions were again on a rollercoaster. Fear, confusion, self-doubt, anger, and frustration were all there, together with a lot off mixed emotions I really did not know I had.

To sit and think clearly at this stage was an exercise that was sometimes impossible. Confusion reigned together with large doses of fear. But what was I afraid of? Well, if they had done this, what was next when they found out that they'd failed? Suppose they fixed my car again. What if they put a bomb in it?

It was during this period that I developed the thought that one really must experience a situation before one can fully understand it. A woman can explain the many emotions, pleasures, and pains of childbirth to a man. But try as he might, he will never really understand it.

Previously, when I had gone to the local police and explained some of the happenings to them, their answer was, "Well, we have good news for you and bad news. The bad news is that with the evidence you have, we can do nothing. The good news is that if anything happens to you, we know where to go looking for the culprit."

I found that very comforting and helpful. I was confident that those out fighting crime and evil were right behind me and in full support!

CHAPTER 5

Though I now lived interstate, my mind often flipped back to and forth to Terri and the picture of her in the driveway as I left.

I reflected on how I had met Terri in the club many months ago, and the funny pants she wore that were in between shorts, culottes, and a skirt. I had never stopped teasing her about that outfit, which used to cause her to become quite indignant until she got to know my sense of humour and when I was winding her up, thereby resulting in a thump on my shoulder.

The club was one of the venues that I used to visit when I was prospecting and wanted to meet ladies looking for love. The supply provided here, together with a pub in the city, proved more than adequate to satisfy the demand for making new friends.

Terri was undoubtedly the best-looking girl there that night, with long fair hair and a very English complexion. She was tastefully but not expensively dressed, except for those pants. She was about five feet two, with probably the nicest legs I had seen on a girl in a long time. I could not take her home because she had come with friends, and they all came in her car, but I made a point of getting her telephone number and arranging to call her later in the week.

In between drinks and dancing I, asked her what she did for a living and whether she was married, divorced, or single. Terri replied, "Well, I am nearly a teacher. I have twelve months to go in college before I am qualified. I decided on teaching after my husband and I separated, and I found myself without a job, no real prospects of getting one, and two boys to bring up."

"So, are you divorced?" I asked.

"Yes, that is all over and settled with. I have been divorced for a while."

"What caused the break-up?" I asked.

"Well, he enjoyed drinking with the boys more than he enjoyed life with me. After a while, I showed him the door. Now, with a grant and working part-time in the kitchen of the hotel across the road, I manage to keep house and home together."

Terrie's was a modest housing commission home that she rented. There had not been a man about the house for a while, and this was obvious. Studying to finish teacher's college and being mum to two young boys kept her busy; there was only so much she could do. The kids were well looked after and not short of love. Despite the boys, the place was always very clean and tidy whenever I was there.

I thought of the time relatively early in the relationship when I planned to meet her one afternoon. I had arranged to pick her up for lunch, and because she had lectures and only had a short lunch break, I thought sandwiches in a local park would be different; we were not far from the college.

As Terri got into the car, she said, "I don't have college this afternoon, so I don't have to be back here, and I've got till five o'clock before I have to be back to pick up the boys. I'm skipping lecture this afternoon."

"OK," I said. "I thought we would grab some sandwiches and go down to the riverbank." I bought some sandwiches and drove to what I thought would be a nice, quiet spot in the park.

It was peaceful when we got there, sunny, and about seventeen degrees, with a light breeze. It wasn't a cold wind; it was a perfect winter's day. We sat in the car whilst we ate lunch and talked. We talked about her and where she was at with her life. We talked about me and where I was at with my life. We got to know more about each other. She was very easy to talk to, if a little nervous. I enjoyed her naivety and found it refreshing.

We were both relaxed—something I had not been able to do for a while. I contemplated a walk along the banks of the river, with the tranquillity of the water broken occasionally by a fish jumping. Where the pleasure boats ply the river, it did provide that. At the park where I was going, it was closer to a muddy little creak, the banks overgrown with weeds and more in its natural setting. It was still pleasant and generally a lot quieter, but not in keeping with the picture that one imagines when talking about the banks of the river.

My fantasy of a peaceful setting was soon shattered by several busloads of young school kids who had arrived and were now running around, yelling and screaming, and chasing each other around the car. The atmosphere I was desperately trying to create was destroyed.

As it worked out, I couldn't have planned it better. I was trying to work out how to get Terri from the park to my unit. So far, Terri had resisted all my previous endeavours, which included candlelit dinners, soft music, barefoot walks along the beach on the sand at night, and trying everything I knew. She always gently told me, "Not now. I'm not ready."

Always the optimist, I said, "Would you like to come back to my place?" To my surprise, Terri agreed. It was about twelve thirty. When we got home, I asked, "Would you like a drink or a cup of tea?"

"Tea, thanks," she said.

As I was making it, I contemplated the success factor of seducing a lady with a cup of Earl Grey served in a chipped coffee mug.

I had known and seen Terri somewhat sporadically for fourteen weeks. More recently, I had seen her several times. I was now at the stage with her that my expectations were not set too high, and so I was taking things slowly—very slowly.

Terri was twenty-seven, and I was thirty-eight. I felt like I was taking advantage of her, which I desperately wanted and was trying very hard to do, but so far, she would not let me. I enjoyed her lack of exposure to the world, the simplicity of what she said, and her genuine honesty. It was a refreshing change. Somewhat cynically, I wondered how much I could think about anyone else's exposure to the real world considering my life at present and the learning curve I was currently experiencing.

Terri was very attractive without being beautiful, with long hair that extended halfway down her back. Her skin was very fair and soft. She had English parents—hardly surprising considering where we lived—and compared to the girls I had taken out since I'd separated from my wife, she was very refreshing.

I had been separated from my wife for about two and a half years, and in that time, I had lost count of the number of women I had been with. I considered myself very lucky with ladies and rarely had difficulty finding a partner when I needed one. But seduction at two in the afternoon on a cup of Earl Grey was, I thought, stretching it.

We had been sitting on the lounge in the lounge room when I put my arm around her and pulled her towards me. Her response was immediate and warm. I remembered that even though she did not have perfume on, her smell lingered and was very pleasant.

"Why don't we go into the bedroom?" I suggested.

"No," said Terri. "What would happen if one of your flatmates came home?"

I had trouble with this because she was prepared to stay in the lounge, which defied logic. "Look, if one of my flatmates did come home, the front door opens right there, about three feet from where we are."

In sheer desperation, I picked Terri up, carried her into his bedroom, and put her on my bed. Her long fair hair spread over his pillow, adding a new dimension to its appearance. For about five seconds, she stayed there. She then sat upright. "What would happen if someone comes home?"

I told her, "No one will be home. They are at work and are out till six o'clock. Until then, no one is going to come home. Besides, they were both free agents, so what the hell."

I pulled her to me and kissed her, lying back on the bed.

She sat upright between kissing many more times before she finally stayed down. I kissed her and nuzzled her neck and her ears. She did not resist when my hand caressed her and moved to cup her breast. One by one, I undid the buttons of her cardigan and eased it back to discover what was causing the interesting shapes when I danced with her on the first night we met.

I started to undress her slowly. In fact, I was doing everything slowly as I enjoyed the moment. I even impressed myself with my control because right now, I wanted to go a lot faster. Her skin was soft and white, and her lack of resistance was evident compared to previous attempts, which caused me to conclude that she was finally ready. Still, I thought I would employ the go-slow strategy.

I noticed the reddening of her neck and the centre of her chest as I looked at her. I kissed her lightly around the neck and slowly moved down, letting my tongue touch her gently on the way. I moved down to her stomach, kissing her lightly and running my tongue softly over her. On the way, I noticed the firmness of her stomach as I unzipped her skirt and slipped it down over her feet.

Her mound, covered by her cottontail pants, made me realise that see-through underwear really wasn't essential because these cottontails actually worked as a turn-on. I brushed aside stupid, distractive thoughts as to how men could ever be homosexual.

Having worked down, I slowly started moving back up, kissing her from her ankles to up between the inside of her legs and over her mound, which I rubbed gently with my nose. I moved to her stomach and then up and over her breasts. I moved from one to the other and let my tongue travel around up and under.

Terri moaned softly and put her hands on my head, pushing me down. I was totally immersed in this world as I looked up to see Terri slowly arching and lowering her body.

I moved down between her legs, nuzzling the soft, fleshy mound and gently nibbling at her. I slipped down her pants at the same time, pulled her legs farther apart, lifted her legs, and dragged her towards me as she guided me into her. All too soon, it was over.

We lay beside each other for a while, talking. I felt that we enjoyed our experience, and so once more I moved on top of her as she wrapped her legs wrapped around me. We went through the process again. Feeling quietly contented, we both lay there and fell asleep

I woke up at just before five. Terri was still asleep, but she'd told me that she had to pick up her kids at five o'clock, and so we had to get moving.

When I woke her, she started with the usual. What would I think of her? Would I lose respect for her? "Do you want to see me again because now you got what you wanted?" I dragged her into the shower and resisted all further urges whilst we showered and got dressed. Time was now against us when I took her back to her car.

While driving back to my flat, I thought about her and our lovemaking. It was then I remembered that in the rush to leave, I had forgotten to make the bed before I had left. My flatmate would be back before I was, and for some reason I did not want them to know I had taken Terri to bed. I was never one to brag about my conquests and believed what went on behind closed doors between two people stayed that way

I was going through some areas of doubt myself and thought I would be a fool to let things develop further. My life was in turmoil at present, and she was so young and innocent, with two young kids to bring up. She already had her hands full.

Did I want to get her involved with the nastiness of my divorce and the uncertainty of what was going on?

CHAPTER 6

n many ways, I was enjoying life. I was seeing several different girls at the same time since I had left my wife. Because of my past experiences I really did not care whether they were married, single, or divorced, or what their ages were. It was a part of the homespun philosophy I had picked up from Doug. "Let them know that you had a number of female friends. Don't lie to them that they are the only one, fall in and out of relationships that last a week or three, and then break up. Just go out, enjoy yourself, see a lot of girls, have fun, and let nature take its course."

This was the philosophy that Doug had used since his wife had been killed in a car accident. I could not fault this approach because I had met dozens of girls since Doug and I had teamed up. I was doing very nicely just sharking on the crumbs that he'd brought home. "The right one will come along, and you will know it when it happens," he said.

I had met Doug at a restaurant. I had taken Leslie, a girl I saw a few times, to dinner, and we were supposed to meet another couple there. They cancelled late, and so Leslie and I were there on our own. During the night, nature called, and so I did what one usually does. Whilst standing there, this character joined me and asked, "Mate, are you living with that bird or just fucking her? We have been watching the pair of you and trying to work it out."

I had a totally twisted sense of humour and broke up laughing. "Well, mate, now I am just fucking her," I said. We then had a few other words of pleasantry. I washed my hands, checked to make sure that I was decent, and went back to the table. I started relating to Leslie the story of what had just transpired in the men's toilet.

Shortly afterwards, Doug came up to us, pulled up a chair, sat down, and started talking to us. He related that he was here with "the Avon lady and some friends", and because we were alone, we could come and join them. We did so and were introduced to the Avon lady, who was Doug's partner for the night; Jane and Cyril; Betty and Malcolm; and another couple whom I never saw again.

Leslie and I were invited to a barbecue at Doug's place the next day.

Sunday was a beautiful, sunny day. We were still somewhat amused at the way we met Doug and his friends, and we were introduced to and somewhat amused by his introduction methodology.

Doug had a large garden set back from the road. There was a pebbled, U-shaped driveway that intercepted a very large front lawn. Many shrubs bordered the driveway, and weeping cherry plants were strategically positioned on the lawn.

Clearly Doug was not short of money. Fenced in the back garden was a swimming pool with a tiled area around it, landscaped to provide a delightful setting for entertaining.

Later, I was to find out the group I was now getting to know was relatively comfortable with their living standards and enjoyed a better than average lifestyle.

When Leslie and I joined the party, we noticed a lot of people there, particularly a lot of seemingly unattached women. After mingling a while and talking to a few of the guests, I spoke to a few of the females to try to establish why the ratio of females to males was so unbalanced. I found out that each of them considered themselves to be Doug's girlfriend.

This left me puzzled, and because Doug was busy cooking and not attending to his guests, I went over and told Doug that I would take over at the barbeque whilst he played host.

Whilst there, Cyril also helped by buttering rolls, getting drinks, and doing all those good things. I related, "Cyril, I have been talking to a few of these ladies here, and they all tell me that they are Doug's girlfriend. What goes on?"

"That's right. All the single ladies at the barbecue are all Doug's friends."

What was more, several were finding out that the other girls knew the layout of the house and the kitchen—and more important were discovering that they were all Doug's girlfriends. None appeared to storm off, and all seemed to be quite happy sharing Doug between them.

Later, when Doug explained his philosophic approach regarding women, I took this philosophy to heart, not knowing at that stage that it would be fifteen years before the right one would come along. But for now, life had become much less complicated as far as women went. I was seeing many women, but all of them were "good friends". Those who wanted it different were put at the back of the call list.

CHAPTER 7

On many occasions after I went interstate to live, my thinking strayed back to some of the actions and difficulties that I had experienced

In many ways, I rued the day that I had gone onto the TV and suggested that if this was the best the legal profession could do with divorce, perhaps it was best handled by someone else. They appeared to be destroying more lives than they saved.

It was the opening of Pandora's box. I thought I was trying to establish a situation to bring about greater equality in divorce, and more important, a better situation for the children affected by it.

There is documentation provided by the government authorities stating that the father should not interfere with this arrangement because he saw so little of the children; discipline was best left to the custodial parent. In other words, dads should butt out.

Deviations from this would confuse the children. It was almost like, "You have done your job bringing the children into the world. Now move over and let the mother do hers.

Get out of the way. Shades off—you have reached your use-by date."

Much later, upon being exposed to the situation I was being subjected to, I thought this was controlled by the lawyers involved with divorce.

I was progressively discovering that the solicitors were but one element in the divorce business, and I was becoming increasingly aware that they were but one cog in the mechanism. I was surrounded by doubts and indecision and found my head in the clouds on more than one occasion.

CHAPTER 8

Many incidences, inexplicable expenses, and situations caused me to think that somehow there had to be more to Christianity then I was experiencing. If another person quoted Job to me, I would crown him with King James. This would not be regarded as a true Christian feeling or attitude, but at this stage, to me Christianity was a learning process.

Being born again was all very new to me, but I doubted this would be regarded as acceptable. I was supposed to be turning the other cheek. That concept was causing me to be hit on both cheeks with much pain, frustration, and outbursts of anger, resulting in the ministers scheduling another counselling session with me.

The ministers were something else, and certainly they had found their true calling. They always left me to make the decisions regarding how I should behave with a little gentle coaxing and guidance from Twiggy and Jim. I could not recall them at any stage saying, "What you did was wrong. You should have done it this way." It was no wonder that the church had grown so quickly. I used to call it the Twiggy factor.

Now I was very heavily involved with the church, to the degree that I was part of a team that went out two by two every Monday evening to invite people to the church on Sunday to meet and become part of the congregation.

I was introduced to Twiggy by a friend who had recently been thrown out of his house by what was now his ex-wife, and who was aware that I was studying the Bible for reasons other than Christian beliefs.

Doug Carling invited me to study the Bible with them, and it went from there.

At that time, I did not understand the importance of what they had taught me and the simple concepts and philosophies that gave me a lot of strength in the ensuing months and years to come. These concepts stayed with me and helped me to stand fast when the pressure was on. I developed a more "by stealth" operation.

CHAPTER 9

One of the members of the Children of Divorce group we had formed visited me one morning and explained how he was a victim of the process and how it was going to cost him his farm. He played for me a tape recording of his five-year-old daughter telling him of the conversation she had overheard. The girl's mother was telling her boyfriend how they were going to take over the farm that had been in his family for generations.

At that stage, he was in his early sixties with a five-year old daughter, so another new start for him would not be easy. This was but one illustration of the system in operation.

Anthony asked his daughter to play the tape, and yes, he heard his wife saying, "I have been told that Anthony is in a position where he cannot pay his bills. He is not paying me maintenance now, and so he is running short of money. If he cannot pay me maintenance or his other bills, he will have to sell the farm to get some money. He cannot work it now, so he has no money coming in. I will have the opportunity to buy the farm. They can arrange it so that it is sold below market value, and I will be able to pick it up at a good price. He will have to sell because now he is running out of money."

"Will you have to sell the farm, Daddy?" asked Simone.

"I don't know, Simone," said Anthony.

At this stage Anthony was in tears. It was a mix of anger and frustration, but this was what he had been reduced to. "Mark, I am in my sixties. I cannot start again and have a family. I could lose my daughter and my farm. That farm has been in my family for generations. How can I rebuild at my age? I cannot have any more children. What will happen if I lose my daughter? It will destroy me."

Anthony's was just one of many stories like this that we had heard.

What the tape did confirm, based on the conversation, was that Anthony had been stopped from working the farm. If he could not work the farm, he had no income and therefore could not pay his bills.

If he couldn't pay his bills, the farm would be sold to pay his debtors. His ex-wife or someone else could then buy the farm, and he would be out.

When he told me this, I did not even begin to understand the mechanisms of the system and how this played a part. But now this situation was being identified as standard operational methodology.

I could understand why Anthony was distraught. This situation was put to him by his five-year-old daughter. To her credit, she had taped the conversation. This understandingly was causing her stress. It was but just one of the stories of this type that I and the members voiced within the group.

We had formed the support group to assist parents and create awareness as to what was going on and how they could help each other. Each of us was now finding out that we were not alone; what had happened to me was happening to others. Progressively, each day we learned more about what we did not know.

Once more, we got out of the square, got off the calf path, and looked at the true picture.

Having started the group, I was also now finding that my mail was being tampered with, cut open, and put back in the letterbox. The contents had obviously been read. Initially we had put this down to the ex-wife gaining evidence for the divorce, but we were past that stage now.

I took this to the state police only to be referred to the federal police, and then I was referred to the local police station. All of them did an excellent impersonation of Pontius Pilate and washed their hands of the situation.

Now, I wasn't so sure so sure. Clearly, we had all assumed that this type of action was part of the divorce, with evidence being collected by private investigators for their wives' solicitors. We had assumed that this was part of the solicitor's methodology to win a case. I was starting to think of other possibilities.

It was becoming increasingly evident that something more was going on, but what? People were always open to the accusation of conspiracy theorists and a myriad of other defamatory accusations.

When I arrived at the office one morning, my secretary was very distressed. "What's the matter, Carol?" I asked.

"When I came in this morning, there was someone in your office. As soon as I came in, they left using your door. I did not think to go and see outside if it was you. I became frightened when I noticed that all the phone receivers were removed from the handset position and placed in a position from top to bottom rather than across the handset cradle."

"Are you all right?" I asked.

"Yes. I was very frightened at first, but I have settled down a bit now."

"Let's call the police," I said.

As soon as the police were advised of this and they identified that a divorce was in progress, they refused to get involved and immediately identified the break-in as a private investigator, not a burglary.

All this time, the group members believed their problems were being caused by their ex-spouses daily. We were identifying that there appeared to be a common methodology or system in place, but by whom? Who or what else was involved? We were being introduced to the possibility that there was more to it, and the solicitors were involved but playing a role.

We identified that the members were being subjected to a high degree of harassment, with expenses being incurred for them at an alarming rate. It put us in a situation whereby we were unable to meet our commitments.

This was fast being identified as a common denominator. Before forming the group, what was happening was that in my case, the debts were incurred on my behalf. The escalation of costs through court hearings, as well as the constant harassment, put me into a situation whereby peace at any cost was a pleasant alternative. Therefore, if an offer was made for my house, and this would stop the pain, it really was a small price to pay for peace and for the whole situation to end. I could get on with life and have some degree of normalcy return.

The emotional and financial turmoil that I was subjected to was comparatively a small price to pay. After talking to others in the group, these thoughts were prevalent and quite common, accepted as the cost of a marriage break-up. We identified that they were being exposed to the same situations of expense creation, false accusations, and what appeared to be common practices in operation. Identifying these practices in isolation would have been impossible and given rise to delusion and paranoia. These symptoms fast disappeared when talking to many other people experiencing the same problems. We realised that we were not alone.

CHAPTER 10

Many years later, after the dust had settled from my divorce and I had put it behind me, I was looking through some old documents and found the sale contract for my house when I was forced to sell it during my divorce

Listed were the names of the buyers. It was listed as a nominee house sale, which meant nothing to me at the time. The name of a couple interstate was listed as the buyer.

I was now somewhat better positioned financially and had the thought that maybe now I could buy back the property from the person named on the contract.

I rang and spoke to her. "My name is Mark. I believe you bought a house interstate some time ago, and I am just ringing to ask you if you still own it and if you wanted to sell it."

She said, "You must be mistaken. Neither my husband nor I have bought a house or anything else interstate. I have never been there, and to my knowledge, neither has my husband."

"Well, the reason I am ringing you is that your name is listed on the sale documents as the buyer. From what you are saying, this is not you. It lists your name, address, and telephone number, which I have just rung."

"Who are you?" she asked.

"My name is Mark. I was the previous owner and used to live there before I moved interstate. I now live locally."

"I think you should talk to my husband, but I am not aware of it. As I say, neither of us has ever been interstate or bought property interstate. Why don't you call him back tonight?"

That night I contacted the husband, and the story was the same. He was a little upset that he had been contacted, and therefore our conversation was quite short and abrupt. I wondered if I had stirred up something between a husband and wife that previously was not there, and so I quickly exited the scene and settled with the statement that this couple was not the party involved, even though the names and address were correct.

It did cause me to do some homework and find out that using a nominee in a property sale was quite common. But who was organising it, and how? At that time, I really was in a quandary. They were listed as the parties having purchased my property, yet they knew nothing about it. When I had the opportunity, I went to the respective government offices and checked the deeds again. They were only listed as the owners for a short time before the property was sold again.

This was when I started checking out the nominee house sale situation and found that this was common practice.

That really was the start of my investigations as to the operations of what I was becoming suspicious about. I had since been advised that this was not allowed in all states, but alternative methods were in place.

Considering all the harassment that I had been subjected to, combined with the similar occurrences that the members of the group, I sought to publicly suggest on TV that perhaps divorce should be taken out of the hands of the legal profession.

The Sunday magazine ran the article in three parts. The first was entitled "The Children of Divorce" by Paul Malarski, with input primarily from a counsellor outlining how children as young as seven were increasingly making their way to psychiatric clinics. These children were torn between two parents attempting to gain maximum gain from settlement.

The second was "Group Hits Out at Legal Loopholes." From this interview, the statement was made abundantly clear that the whole system was up the creek because the children were torn between two parents. The counsellor went on to say that she did not want to have anything more to do with it; it sickened her. There was nothing she could do about it. It was all in the hands of the lawyers trying to win a case regardless of the human element involved. She had seen people become paranoid while defending themselves against affidavits that were completely wrong. *A funny coincidence,* I thought.

The newspapers then went on to cite the views of the then president from the Law Society in article three; "Panel's Absurd Idea: Lawyer", stating that the use of panels was totally absurd and denigrating the concept.

I had experienced this on more than one occasion in my own experiences, as well as with members within the group.

Today, fathers were being accused of interference with their children. This type of tag stuck when I was involved, and it sticks today. Whether true or false, the father is branded.

The people I spoke to have the same opinion as I: this was a despicable act that they would not even contemplate, and to be branded for an untruth of this kind was despicable. Who is the blame for this? Is this the system? Or is it just some members of the legal profession who have made this a part of the system? How much of this is generally known within the industry and accepted as part of the system? If this is accepted as part of the system, this must include the relative government bodies and the legal profession.

Lawyers may be doing their job, but they were causing trouble. If they were causing trouble, then perhaps it shouldn't be their job.

In summation, the counsellor indicated that lawyers and judges did not understand how these matters could affect people. These were the words spoken by a councillor, published at that time in the daily papers.

The second article was based on the discussion with the group, formed by Tony and me, stating that it was time for an overhaul to the family court system. The claim was that the lawyers, with their "win at all costs" attitude, were forcing men to turn their backs on ridiculous maintenance and custody settlements to seek a new life interstate.

From me, they were seeking eight hundred dollars a month, and that was in the early eighties. This was after putting me in a situation where I had no income.

Add to this the process of psychological warfare destroying a lot of parents, causing them to turn their backs and walk away from their families. Also, at that time there was a letter to the editor confirming my belief that the innocent parties that suffered most were the children in both the long and short term. They felt guilt that they were the cause of the break-up, and they became the pawns and lost both parents.

I had released a monster. From that point on, there was a higher incidence of people entering my flat and somebody else's body odour in my flat. However, there was nothing I could really pin it to but feelings.

Constantly, expenses were incurred for me, including legal fees that I could not meet; arrangements I made with creditors were set aside. I traced some of this back to a solicitor named Yourdon. There was no relation to the one with the same name representing my wife. I obtained this information from the manager of the mercantile company with which I had made the arrangements. I had met every payment on time. Why were they changed? It was then that the manager told me he did not know why, but he was instructed to do so by his superiors on instructions from Yourdon.

This was the methodology used to win a case. Why? What was their objective? At this stage, I still could not determine how my activities in this arena caused Theo to threaten me as he did. More important, what was the connection between people going through a divorce and Theo? Why was I threatened if I went ahead with our campaign on television and with the media?

From what I had seen of the process, I and other members of the group were being subjected to common procedures, or a system. But only some played this game, so how did we identify the main players, and what were the ground rules? Who were the players? What were the qualifying factors to be allowed to play? All I had were a lot of questions with very few answers and even fewer facts.

Clearly the two divorcing parties formed opposing teams. They then enlisted their respective legal representatives. If children were involved, they became part of the game or the prize for winning.

If you win custody, you win unilateral control and the greater percentage of the joint assets. Any property, money, assets, or business assets of any description form part of the pool.

A fee for playing the game was paid to legal representatives, irrespective of the results.

Sometime later, I asked myself, "Was there a percentage of their fees being paid to an organiser or controller? Was, as I thought, this part of an age-old system whereby they make excellent money but are required to pay a percentage to a higher party? Was this what Theo was afraid of my finding out? Was he an organiser or an operative of the system? Where did he fit?" His European descent implied some knowledge unknown to me at the time. Always I had questions.

The two divorcing parties always lost, one more than the other. The children lost a parent and financial stability, and they won the erroneous feeling of rejection, being unwanted, and the position of a pawn between the two parties. This situation has long-term effects for parents' lives and for their children's lives. The long-term effects went on for generations, and the psychological effects on children of divorce could be seen every day.

Increasingly, I was becoming aware that the divorcing parents really did not know or understand the game being played, who the players were, and what their involvement was. They were doing what they were told. They were encouraged to develop an increasing distrust of their ex. This was easy because neither party was really communicating with the other. Communication had long since broken down before a separation occurred, and so communication generally was not good.

What had been established? Protracted divorce situations with conferences, court appearances, and additional fees earned with a now healthy growing adversarial situation. This went to the legal profession. Really, we wanted to them to "win" the situation for us. We were too emotionally embroiled to realise that winning was not an achievable outcome. One lost more than the other, but both were losers.

At best, one (usually the custodial parent) got a greater share of what was left of the assets. This was almost always given to the wife because she was better equipped to handle the situation and bring up the children properly, wasn't she?

Frustration of access, one of the tools used, caused intense animosity between the parents and appeared to be fostered by the solicitors. The non-custodial parent blamed the custodial parent, and no doubt the custodial parent would have to share some of the blame for this, if only for going along with it.

With hindsight, some of this could be complete ignorance on their behalf. But hey, we could not agree when we were married, and my ex was not behaving the way I thought she should, so why not? Each of the divorcing parties had an emotional mix of feelings.

From what we could determine, this was contrived and fostered. Who was responsible for this situation, the divorcing parties, the solicitors, or the system? Who was the only person who, for a small consideration, would relieve you of all your problems and allow you to set about the all-important task of rebuilding your life? Who was best positioned to throw oil on these troubled waters?

Who had you just appointed to take up the cudgel for you, together with his experience and your cooperation? Because if you don't give it to him, he will not represent you. They set to this with a will.

Initially, I used to lay all the blame on the solicitors. It took me years to establish that they were only part of the operation and were being controlled. Furthermore, not all the legal profession worked this system's methodology. Some I spoke to were very critical of those who did.

Easy payment loans were made to the potential custodial parent by the banks, with the payback to be made after settlement and assets sold.

At this stage, I did not realise just what I was stumbling into—the sheer enormity and sophistication of the situation. Was it fact or a figment of my vivid imagination from a mind already screwed by the rigours of divorce? It was a situation increasing daily in today's world.

CHAPTER 11

I wondered at the sheer size and scope of what I theorised was a beautiful structure whereby the losing parties were the warring parents, and they had set about their own destruction. From what I saw, it was a brilliant piece of machinery. If my theorising was accurate, I could only marvel at the finesse and ingenuity of the operators.

Here, under the noses of society, was a wonderfully intricate piece of organisational machinery that embraced all levels of business, society, and the legal profession—and it was unknowingly supported by the government.

I initially thought I was getting carried away with my theorising and imagining things. This was just too fantastic for words. One only read about these things or saw them in the movies.

But what I and many others had experienced over the last few months and years was no movie.

At first, I thought that I was imagining things and my imagination was too vivid. Progressively over time, in between thinking that I was losing it, funnies occurred. It was happening to me. If I was right—and daily, I was being given evidence that I was—here was a revenue stream generating millions of dollars.

I initially experienced this process in the early eighties, when I was going through my divorce. As such, I estimated that if my thoughts were right, here was a million-dollar moneymaking mechanisation that was operating under the cloak of a legitimate operation.

But all I had at that time was from a mind that was being subjected to a divorce situation, when under no circumstances could one's thinking be regarded as entirely rational.

What was the ceiling? I discovered this operation in one state. Progressively, I discovered that my suspicions were proving to be correct and that it was operating in all states.

The income stream from the money paid to solicitors, investigators, and all the other cling-ons—what a moneymaking machine!

At that stage, I did not truly understand the length, breadth, and scope of what I was starting to believe. I was initially looking at it purely from the position of one being divorced. I was looking at it from my situation, from my viewpoint. My thinking was obviously clouded—back and forth again, between right and left brain with one affecting the operation of the other. Emotions and logic were strange companions.

As I followed this train of thought, I started extrapolating the figures and guessing on numbers of divorces per annum and value of assets. The more went on, the more it explained the funnies' in the flat; the opening of my mail, and the strange happenings surrounding me. But I was still having difficulty trying to get my mind around the concepts of just what I was starting to think but not really believe.

What I thought I had stumbled into was one thing. The level of people involved was another. If I was right, it had to involve a cast of thousands, if Harrigan Yourdon and Lowe were involved. Harrigan was a friend of Tony Bradshaw, a former chartered accountant who had left the practice and gone into politics. Could this explain why I got so little assistance from Bradshaw when I visited him?

My bank manager was very helpful when I spoke to him, and he advised me that the directive to freeze my bank account had come from the head office. I could understand this. But after the meeting I had with the manager in the head office, I could not understand it at all and felt the behaviour was nothing short of strange.

The man appeared to be uncomfortable when I went to see him, and he was afraid of something. I felt that his whole manner and demeanour was not what I'd expected.

Based on these theories, thoughts, ideas, and concepts floated through my mind. However, all I had were concepts and theories. Apart from the inexplicable of what had been happening to me, there was nothing concrete.

CHAPTER 12

On one of the last discussions with my ex-wife as to what she was doing and her behaviour before our separation, she insisted that she was not doing anything that other married women were not doing.

Based on this and the other governing factors, I decided that my marriage was over. I must have been one hell of a bad lover, husband, and provider.

I left my wife and took a flat. In order to test my wife's words that she was not doing anything that other married women were doing, I decided that my field of research would be best conducted in clubs and a variety of hotels. For that matter, I'd go anywhere where women collected. In the cause of science, pleasure, and a large portion of ego and self-esteem rebuilding, I went to work.

I decided to find out just how true my wife's statement was. To do this, I was going to need to experiment. I took to this with a will. I did random sampling in all areas: married, single, separated, divorced, young, and old. A skirt or female legs in pants was fair game.

From these experiments, I concluded that my wife was right. I did not consider myself to be any oil painting, and the ratio was proving to be about 75 per cent of married women freelancing. It gave me a very cynical view of the world and a very biased outlook on women. But for every woman that was out freelancing, there had to be a man. The figure still staggered me.

On one occasion, when I was out prospecting,' I ran into the wife of one of my salesmen. This caused her to go into "Please do not say anything to Harry" mode. I agreed—if she came into the car park with me for half an hour.

Long ago I had decided, perhaps naively, that once married, taking other women to bed was a no-go. Forget the moralistic situation; that was another issue on its own. But, being the creatures, we are, all that infidelity did was confuse the issues within a marriage, and if one had a problem within one's marriage, sleeping with someone else outside of it did nothing to alleviate the situation.

I also discovered that to many people, sleeping with someone else whilst married often did not mean they wanted the marriage to end. All it meant was that for any one of a dozen reasons, they had the hots for someone else, and it was a purely physical situation. In fact, for a while I still wore my wedding ring and found out from many ladies that I could go out and have some fun knowing that there were no strings attached. Well, in theory anyway. Yeah, well, so much for my beliefs. That was now due for rapid revision, and I was firmly convinced that a large percentage of married females I associated with from my random sampling batch, were freelancing.

The reasons I heard were many and various as to why they got married. They wanted to have children, wanted to go through university and wanted a companion. Towards the end, I would throw my notebook down and tell them to write their details down, and I would get back to them.

Mixed with large doses of scotch and soda, I promptly forgot who those names were the next day, what they looked like, or from where I got the names. I put the thoughts of fidelity into the land of the Easter bunny and Santa, strictly for the belief of the young and naïve; it was something that one grew out of.

Now I had to face up to the situation I now found myself in, as well as the accuracy of the accusations of naivety.

CHAPTER 13

Tony and I started Children of Divorce. Our concentration was on the situation that non-custodial parents were in and how it affected us and our children—nothing more.

Always the question remained: how did this effect Theo? What was I supposed to know, or what did I already know? Whatever I supposedly knew, I was unaware of it. So in some respects, thank you, whoever you are. You thought I knew more than I knew, and as such, you are giving me the treatment. You put the fear of God into me for a long time. Good, old-fashioned FUD.

But fear diminishes over time. Fear is generated by a catalyst; this was caused by you. Cognitive bolstering by me took over from there to become a self-defeating and demoralising influence; this was done by me to me.

I let my thoughts wander to what might happen or what accident might befall me because of what they thought I knew and how I was going to use that knowledge to destroy their plans, go public and, interfere with whatever they had put into place. I wished I knew whatever the hell that was. Now, some of the pennies started to drop into place.

From where I sat, I thought I knew diddly squat, and proving anything concrete was not within the realms of possibility. I had a lot of theories, deductions, and thoughts but no proof. So, what was this all about? As far as fact, I had very little, apart from calculated thoughts based on the happenings over time and expectations of the cost to maintain this harassment for as long as they did. Clearly whoever they were, they were unaware of the reality of the true situation. But they feared what I did know or what damage I could do.

Once more, fear was the driving force, or was it money, or revenge, or eleventy seven other bloody possibilities that I had not, could not, figure out. Looking at the potential reasons for the harassment, I had to include more than just Theo and his operation. As my solicitor said, hell hath no fury.

I established a rumour that I had committed everything to writing and tape, and if anything should happen to me via a sudden and unforeseen accident, the writings would surface. On it were dates, names, places, examples—the full story.

This action triggered a spate of more visitations to my flat and my girlfriend's houses, with them asking me serious questions about my background.

On one occasion when Anita, one of my lady friends, stayed with me overnight, she rang me to tell me that as she was driving home from my place the next morning, she found her car difficult to control through loss of traction. The back slid everywhere. We looked at where it had been parked that night to discover oil had been placed on the rear tyres. There was oil on the floor of the garage.

This frightened the hell out of her and brought about another series of questions. "What's going on with you? Who would do this? What haven't you told me about you? Who are you tied up with?"

It also confirmed to me that someone other than me could access my garage—another one of the funnies that I had experienced. It brought the question that if this was Theo, why this? What was the connection. Should I look at someone else trying to get even with me?

Anita was not alone. Other ladies whom I had been out with indicated that they had thought someone had entered their houses. This put the fear of God into them for themselves and for their children. When I attempted to explain that I thought I was being harassed and that this was happening as part of the harassment, all I did was instil more fear in them.

In addition, I management to convince them that I was paranoid, totally off my trolley, and set for permanent residency at the funny farm, further adding to the situation.

To say I was in a downward spiral would be an understatement. As I had discovered, some funny things had happened to me, but they had happened to me—I could not show what had happened to anyone else. If I could have taken a picture and shown that to people, I was confident that they would believe me.

But there are some things you just cannot photograph. When I tried to explain, "I am being harassed. There are people entering my flat and doing strange things to me," I would get questions like "Who would do that?" I'd say, "I don't know for sure. I think it could be my ex-wife or the Europeans." I could see the disbelief in their faces.

People started to doubt me and what I was saying, so I stopped talking about it. I knew that my not being able to talk and my internalising brought about other problems. It also brought home to me that I was primarily under the belief that it was Theo responsible for the funnies. But was there someone else as well?

Always the question remained: "Are you playing with yourself again, boyo? If so, stop and look at yourself."

To verify my sanity, I started taking stock. I was broke but for the good graces of a couple of ladies. I would be adequately credentialed to apply as a candidate for the queue at the soup kitchen. I was so broke and in debt, with my confidence at a minus factor, that I decided I was overdue to put myself back together again and totally rebuild.

I managed to get a job in sales in the computer industry. On the weekends, I sold real estate. Using this combined income, I slowly started repaying the debts I owed, and I repaid the faith that some people had put in me.

CHAPTER 14

When I got home from work one night, I decided that it was time to get serious in relation to determining what was fact, fantasy, delusions, or stupidity. I wanted to know what was going on and determine whether I was insane or partway to losing it. I started to write,

When did the funnies start?
My flat in Camden? No,
When I was renting Matt's house? No.
I felt that I really became aware of it when I was living alone. At all the other locations, I was sharing accommodation with somebody else or was unaware. The first time it happened; I was on my own.

What were the funnies?
Someone had been into my flat. Initially it was nothing I could put my finger on, just a feeling. Unusual smells like body odour, or things not being where I put them or disappearing totally.

My mail was cut open and placed back in the letterbox. The only tangible was the mail. I could see, feel, and touch envelopes that had been cut open and put back in my mailbox.

Going to the police was a waste of time.

Was my office entered during this period?
Yes, it was, when I was living at Camden.
So, from what I could remember, it all started when I was living at Camden as far as the office went. But in my flat, I only became aware of it when I was living alone.

What I did discover was that I arranged the unit at Camden through a friend, Anne. She was living a few doors away from my wife and me, and they had been close friends. Anne was providing my ex-wife with several details of my accommodation—payment history and heaven knew what else.

Isolating fact from fiction was an interesting experiment. It was proven that someone had entered my office; the police and my assistant could attest to that. I accepted that as fact.

Whatever the hell fact was, somewhere in my reading I had discovered that according to scientific axiom, "There is no such thing as fact; there is hypothesis supported or not supported by evidence." Oh, good. I really needed that right now. It created further confusion. So, what evidence could I muster?

During the separation process, divorce was established. So that was, as I believed, my wife's solicitor gaining evidence.

During this period, I believed that I was getting interference at work. Because my wife's solicitor had stopped me from using our house as security for the business, I was now battling to keep it going. Arrangements with creditors were being kept.

Someone had uncoupled that arrangement. The coincidence was that that someone had the same name as the solicitor being used by my wife.

I ran into the manager of the mercantile agency in the city one day and asked him, "Carl, what is going on? You and I had an arrangement, and I have stuck to that. Why have the ground rules changed?"

"Mark, I have been instructed by my manager in the head office to do this. I had no choice. He was contacted by a solicitor named Yourdon. Do you know him?"

"I don't know," I said. "He has the same name as my wife's solicitor."

"Well, he was the one who brought about the change. Apparently, you have some debts with some other people that he is trying to chase up. Mark, I am glad we met here because I have always found you to be straight up and down, so I am telling you this. I could not repeat or say this in the office."

This tied in with what my bank manager had told me when he had to close my company account.

In both cases, the managers had been given instructions from their superiors and were following instructions. They shared information unofficially, and when I followed it up with their superiors, I found the behavioural characteristics incongruent. I suspected fear in their actions. Initially I thought I was imagining things.

More evidence gathering by my wife's solicitor. Why? They had me on the ropes now. What were they after?

A combination of these events left me in a state of confusion with a large amount of fear, and I was financially rocky.

Through a variety of different methods, subtle, psychological games were being played, creating a high degree of doubt. Talking to the authorities proved pointless, as were the politicians. Police did not or could not act.

Friends simply did not believe me. To try to create awareness was rebounding on me. All I did was create doubt with others about me. This was counterproductive. There was more than enough doubt in my mind as to what the situation was. Having suggestions of doubt cast by outsiders did nothing to help and only caused further confusion and doubt.

In this state of uncertainty that I could feel myself sinking into, I decided to make a list of the funnies and the many thoughts going around in my mind. It was only when I started writing this down that clarity became possible.

The Events
My Belief
The Relevant Consequence

Some Events
My office entered—When did it start?
          Personal items missing or moved in flat.
          Strange smells when I entered my flat or car.
Body odour—not mine, acetate.
          Mail opened and put back in letterbox;
          clean cut.
          Clock in the car not having worked for
          a couple of years, and then one morning

working and within a minute or two of the correct time.

What appeared to be an aerial attached to the wheel arch of the car. No mechanic could provide an explanation.

Underwear placed in a recycling bag appears back in my wardrobe.

Seat position in car changed by somebody.

Belief

My ex-wife's divorce solicitors employing investigators to obtain divorce evidence.

When I was living at Camden—divorce getting dirty.

Investigators looking for something— what? They had me on the ropes for my divorce. Harassment? They did not give a toss that I knew I was under surveillance.

Consequence

Established fact: intruder disturbed by my secretary, a witness.

Confirmed office; flat still unsure, though I believed so.

Started set things up in my flat and recording it so that if it had been moved, I would know.

Confirmed things were moved.

Took to police—a waste of time.

When did the funnies start? Or more important, when did I start becoming aware of it?

I became increasingly aware of this when I was living alone. The only person I could talk to was the guy up top who carried a shepherd's crook, but because he did not answer back in many ways, or in the ways I was used to, was he even listening?

I did establish that I noticed the funnies before and after the divorce proceeding was well under way. That was when the rules changed. I thought it might have been going on long before, but I was unaware of it. Now I was on full alert. What was the trigger that brought about change?

I had been on TV and started to talk about taking divorce out of the hands of the legal profession, particularly in its current format. On reflection, was this the catalyst? Or was this my ex-wife's doing?

The situation did not change when I went interstate to live.

Once I had clearly established that I was not hallucinating, losing it, or ready for the funny farm, I went back home and employed two private investigators to investigate me. At least from this, I was starting to put a peg in the ground.

This was one of the most effective actions that I took to enable me to move forward, establish the cause of the funnies, and confirm that I was not losing it. They identified that I had a problem, and they identified Theo. Somebody else had seen and was aware of the situation.

CHAPTER 15

Until this time, I blamed the solicitors; my anger was directed at them, my ex-wife, and many combinations in between. They were the ringleaders, the masterminds behind the system or methodology. They had engineered the situation to their benefit. They were the clouds that got in the way.

The session with Theo threw a whole new light onto the situation. Clearly there was a level above the solicitors, an angle I'd never considered. They were but one part of the mechanism

I again started reviewing just what I was doing, or had done, that could affect Theo. I'd started Children of Divorce with the prime intent to create public awareness and bring about a change in relations between custodial and non-custodial parents.

This situation was aggravated by some members within the legal profession specialising in divorce who became somewhat zealous in how they proceeded within this arena. To paint the entire legal profession as the perpetrators would be inaccurate and misleading. But who were in or out?

It was a closed shop, with the profession guarding their own. Comparing their actions as to how large numbers of the legal profession portrayed the father in a divorce situation was beyond my understanding, particularly with the vilification they practiced. But to put all solicitors under this cloak would be misleading. Several I spoke to were not and did not want to be involved in that situation, even though they were aware of it.

I had appeared on television and radio, suggesting that perhaps divorce should be taken out of the hands of the legal profession.

The surveillance stupidity really came home to me on one occasion when I was asked to conduct a communications course in a couple of interstate cities. I arranged to do the farthest one first. That night, on the way back to the second city, I had bought a packet of Smarties, which I had only half eaten; I'd put the half-full box on top of my clothes in my suitcase.

On arriving at the motel, I went to unpack my suitcase to find that the Smarties were spread throughout my clothes. The empty box was at the bottom of the suitcase. Given the way the Smarties were throughout my clothes, it became obvious that this was not the rigours of air travel. Someone had opened the suitcase, lifted the box of Smarties, and sprinkled them throughout the folded clothes.

This could only have happened during the time when my suitcase was in the possession of the airline baggage handling crew. At all other times, the suitcase was in my possession from the motel to the airport and again from the airport back to the motel.

How could I explain that to people? Was it a gentle reminder saying, "We know you are in town, and you are being watched"?

Before the meeting with Theo, I had thought I was losing it and had gone through a myriad of feelings: doubt, paranoia, and insecurity. I now had it confirmed that I was quite sane, a lot disillusioned, and somewhat bitter and withdrawn.

I did not know what I was supposed to know. All he knew was that I was under surveillance and was being harassed. My flat was being entered at will, expenses were being incurred for me, and the reality was that I was not able to get on with my life and forget the past.

Getting on with life was becoming quite a challenge. I would form relationships with girls, and somewhere along the way things would go awry. One was a Swedish lady named Barbara. I met her at a singles party whilst I was out prospecting. She had been married before and had two daughters, one at university and one still at school—or to use an expression common at that time, a latchkey child. A few weeks after we met, she got the feeling that someone had been into her house on more than one occasion, which was causing her to question me, my background, my history and whom had I upset.

Over the course of the next few weeks, I explained to her that I thought it might be harassment that I was experiencing. She too joined the other potential ladies that I had seen and was concerned for her daughters' safety. After a short time, we called it quits and went our separate ways. I was quite keen on her and was a quite upset by the break-up.

At this stage, I was living in a unit right on the waterfront. The unit overlooked the harbour, right in line with the southern pylon of the bridge. On the Saturday night following the break-up, I was sitting on the veranda with a glass of red wine and a cup of coffee, feeling a little low. I heard a male voice calling out, "Barbara? Barbara, where are you?"

This was called out a couple of times, and I heard someone laughing and talking to someone else. Then there was silence.

It was a very quiet night with only the sounds of the ferries going past occasionally. When the voice called out, it was unmistakable. Was it a mistake? Was I hearing things? Was it a coincidence?

Always a series of who, what, and why went through my mind, and the doubts and uncertainties started again.

This was not the first time that something of this nature had happened in previous relationships. Another lady, this time with a young son, indicated that she thought her house had been entered on more than one occasion. Again, I was questioned as to my background, and that relationship also ended with fear on her side as to what I was or had been involved with. Once more, as soon as I told her what I felt the situation was, the relationship ended.

On reflection, this situation had happened before several times—in fact within twelve months after coming back from interstate. During this time, I was ringing Terri frequently and corresponding with her. We decided that she and her two boys would come to live in Interstate with me. I rented a house, Terri and the boys came over, and we set up house. On more than one occasion, Terri thought she heard someone downstairs through the night and thought it was one of the boys. Likewise, when I heard it, I also put it down to the boys.

On one occasion, Terri checked the boys, and they were both sound asleep. Explaining to Terri what I thought it had been convinced her that I was paranoid. Terri came with me when I went and spoke to a shrink. This turned out to be fruitless because he simply did not understand.

Needless to say, that was another relationship that ended. The similarity on these situations often made me wonder whether my ex-wife was involved in the harassment or the funnies.

These things happened to me. I saw the car clock work again after not having worked for a couple of years. I saw and picked up the Smarties distributed through my clothes in my suitcase. I and the mechanic saw a cut tyre that he said was not an accident.

But regrettably, I could not show these events to anyone, and talking to anyone about it was an exercise in futility.

CHAPTER 16

Shortly after the break-up with Barbara, I heard from my father that my stepmother had passed away, and he was now living on his own,

After he told me this, I made a point of going over and seeing him on Friday evenings and staying overnight, doing little things with and for him and his house.

My father lived in a two-bedroom house that was looking a little worse for wear. I painted the kitchen, laundry, and lounge rooms and recarpeted the dining area. He was in his eighties, seldom drank, and lived for his bowls and a quiet life.

I had been living interstate for several years, and so I was out of contact with him and my family. On these Friday nights, now that I was back living in the same state, having a quiet meal together gave us the opportunity to talk and reconnect.

I had always been close to my father, from the time my parents separated until my transfer interstate. I made a point of seeing him whenever I came to where he lived, even if only for a short time.

It was on one of these Friday evenings that my father mentioned to me that he used get calls at strange times through the night or early morning, between two and three o'clock in the morning. They would not say anything but wait for a minute and then hang up. It was long enough for him to know that there was someone there because he could hear breathing.

On other instances, he was woken up by someone outside his bedroom window calling out his name, Jimmy, and then laughing. He thought that was unusual because to a lot of friends, he was known as Eddie.

He was known as Jimmy by family and people who knew him from his childhood, as well as when he was overseas.

On one occasion, he came home to find newspapers rolled up as if to be set alight and placed under and around his house. To a man in his eighties, this caused him some concern. As such, he slept with a wrench near his pillow.

I mentioned this to my relatives, who immediately dismissed it as my father being delusional. However, on more than one occasion when I was there; I was awakened by the phone ringing, answered it before my father, and received the same treatment.

This happened before I had brought it up with the family. Therefore, I knew that there was nothing delusional about being woken up at some ungodly hour by a phone ringing.

Was I delusional as well? Voicing my protests to them turned out to be futile. I too had also received similar calls and was constantly woken up at strange times early in the morning. Was there any connection?

I thought, *What the bloody hell did Theo have to do with my father? Was this someone else?* It was back to the wise men. I quietly filed it away, and on subsequent visits, my father and I would often discuss it to establish who it could be and why.

We went through several alternatives. I always remembered my mother instilling in me the concept "If your mind can conceive it, you can achieve it" and "Never take no for an answer". Was it one of my relatives or anyone inside the family, and why?

After several sessions of this nature, my father casually mentioned that it could have been his superannuation money. This comment left me nonplussed. "What superannuation money, Dad?" I asked.

"Well, when we had to leave the colonies after they got independence; I could not take my super out of the country, and so it has been there unclaimed all this time."

My mother and father had lived in one of the British colonies for many years until they gained independence from the UK. Therefore, having lived there for as long as he did, when he was in the army, superannuation was accruing. When they left to go to the UK, the government would not allow my father to take out his money.

"Would you like me to investigate it?" I asked.

"How could you do that?"

"Well, I have dealings with the high commissioner's office during my business activities. I could ask them when I am there next time."

"Well, if you can do it."

"I might need a letter of authorisation," I said. "If so, I will come back to you."

I was in the high commissioner's office soon after and asked him, "Amal, my father left your country after they got independence from the UK. When he left, he was not allowed to take his superannuation with him. He tells me he has never claimed it. What are the chances of claiming it now, and how do I go about it?"

"Mark, you would stand an excellent chance of getting that superannuation money now. Heavens, yes, it would be worth pursuing. You would stand an excellent chance of getting it. After all this time, it would be worth over a million dollars now. I suggest that you pursue it. If you need any assistance, let me know, and I will see what we can do for you here. Is your father still alive?"

"Yes. He knows I am talking to you about it."

On the following Friday evening, when I was at my father's place, I said to him, "Pop, I was talking to the commissioner's officer during the week, and he indicated to me that we should pursue your superannuation money. He suggested that we may need an international lawyer, but he also indicated that it would be worth over a million dollars in today's terms. What do you want me to do? Do you want me to start recovery procedures?"

My father was in somewhat of a shock when I told him the amount, but he readily agreed for me to commence recovery.

A few weeks later, another relative, Stephan, was visiting my father. During that visit, some discussion must have taken place because on the next visit to my father, he indicated to me that after talking to Stephan and his wife, they convinced him not to pursue the money because it would affect his pension.

I had trouble with this logic because if my father gained one million dollars plus at his age, he would not need the pension or anything else and could live his later years in complete financial security. But that was the decision, and so I let it rest.

Shortly after another visit by Stephan, I received the call from my father saying that he was trapped under his wardrobe. He asked if I could come free him.

I left the office immediately, but it was some time before I got to my father's house because he was about an hours' drive from the office. On arrival, my father greeted me at the door and explained that fortunately, the neighbour had called in to see how he was and had released him.

My father explained that Stephan had rearranged the bedroom furniture for him during his last visit, and when he went to put something on top of the wardrobe, he had pulled it down on himself.

"Pop, I'm intrigued. You have been doing this for years. What's different? Show me."

In demonstrating this to me, the wardrobe started toppling down on him again. Fortunately, I could stop it and pushed it back into position.

Knowing that this was my father's habit and he had not experienced anything like this before, I checked the positioning of the wardrobe to find the back of the robe was resting on the skirting board and as a result was not level on the floor. The action of my father in pulling on the top of the wardrobe, as he used to do, would cause it to tip forward. Once I had placed it on the floor and the wardrobe was on level ground, it was stable. We went through the process many times to ensure that it did not happen again.

My father was in his eighties, quite slim, and now frail. He had been diagnosed with cirrhosis and was being treated accordingly. This always caused me some amusement because my father was no drinker. Though a member of the local services club, he rarely drank alcohol. When bowling, he would sit on a pony, which was about as small a glass of beer as one could get. His only outings were to the club and back.

Some months after this incidence, again after a visit from Stephan, I received a call at the office from my father asking to be taken to the hospital; there was no rush, just when I could get there. The CEO's secretary, who had taken the call, came to see me and told me that the CEO told me to go now. All of them were aware of the situation between my father and me.

When I got there, we had something to eat and set off. Urgency was not stressed. I took my father to the hospital outpatients together with a letter given to my father from his doctor.

Shortly after two attendants came out and placed him on a gurney. They scolded, telling me that my father should have been brought in hours ago. He was going to be admitted and would need all his toiletries, a change of underwear, and all relevant requirements for a long stay in hospital. I had to go get them whilst they admitted him and made him ready for treatment.

I was a little stunned because although my father had been talking about feeling unwell last week, he said he was feeling quite well until the last few days.

Somewhat confused, when I returned later, I was told that my father was seriously ill and might not come out of hospital. I was told to advise any relevant members of the family of the situation.

He had been placed in what they classed the terminally ill ward. He had been sedated, and so although I could see him, he could not talk or recognise me. I sat with him until about eight o'clock that night, and then I decided to spend the night at my father's place. My mind operated at the lighting speed of a wounded tortoise.

That night and the next morning, I rang the family to advise them of the situation. I thought that I must be as thick as a brick. How did I not see my father's situation? I saw him every weekend. How did I not see my father's condition worsening?

The family started arriving. That evening, we all went to a restaurant and had a meal. It was decided that the oldest should take on the responsibility for my father's affairs, and the oldest brother was also the executor. This was agreed to by all. I really could not give a toss one way or the other.

The next day, whilst at the hospital, Stephen's wife approached me to tell me that she had arranged for the next-door neighbour to dispose of all the perishables in my father's refrigerator.

I was a little surprised because they knew I was staying there, but on the scale of priorities, this ranked about eleventy seven. That was until I went home to find that the only perishables that had been removed were the things cooked by Maryanne for my father on their last visit—the week before he had to be admitted to hospital.

The other perishables were still in the fridge. At this stage, no significance was put on it until many months afterwards.

Much later, the penny dropped, and I remembered that on the previous visit Stephan and Maryanne had made, my father had stopped me from pursuing the money. On a subsequent trip, he'd pulled the wardrobe down on himself. Was there any connectivity?

The next-door neighbour just happened to call in to see if he was all right. After the last trip, my father was hospitalised, regarded as a very sick man, and placed in a terminally ill ward in hospital. Once more, I had some funnies. Were they a long line of coincidences? Was I seeing things that were not there?

Added to this, I had received the telephone calls at my father's house. I listened for a while, and they hung up. This was not imagined or a coincidence. Was I being suspicious over nothing? Was the same person who was harassing me also harassing my father? Was there any connection?

After a few days, after my father was admitted to hospital, my nephew and I were on the night shift. We were playing a game of cards when my father made some noises— or as much as he could, with the pipe stuck in his mouth. I was quite distraught to see my father in this situation, and I prayed that my father would be taken. I also said to my father, "Pop, let go. You do not enjoy being like this. Stop hanging on. Let go."

Shortly afterwards, my father gave his last gasp. My nephew and I waited a few minutes and then called the nurse. She came in shortly and confirmed that he had passed away.

The nurse asked me what I wanted to do. I asked her if she could remove the tube from his mouth, wash him, tidy him up, and call me back so that the last picture I had of him was a peaceful one. The nursing staff did an excellent job, and when they called me back, they had removed the tube from his mouth. Obviously, they'd washed him and laid him out so that the last picture I had of him was very peaceful, as if he was asleep. I was the person who'd brought him into the hospital and was recorded as the next of kin, and so they collected all his belongings and gave them to me.

It was after midnight when we left the hospital. I went to the motel where some of my relatives were staying and told them the news. At the same time, I dropped off my nephew and went to tell my mother and sisters, who were staying at my father's house. Sleep was not an option for me at that time, and so I decided a quick ride into the city for a pancake and a coffee. I stayed there until about seven the next morning and then headed back home.

A little later, a couple of us returned to the hospital to officially identify the body and commence funeral arrangements. They came to me to identify the body, and at the same time they advised me that because they could not identify the cause of death, they could not release the body straight away until a post-mortem had been performed.

I was a little nonplussed by all of this. My father had been in hospital under their care and treatment for some time. My belief was that they were treating him for an ailment, and that was the cause of his death. If not, what was? But that was the situation, and we could do nothing about it.

The night that my father died, I was given my father's personal belongings. Somewhere along the way, I had opened my father's wallet to see what was in there. On a piece of paper, on the top right-hand side, was a figure of one hundred thousand dollars. Going down the page, I saw the names of the relatives: for one, twenty thousand dollars; another got fifteen thousand; for me, fifteen thousand; and so on. The figures amused me because I had, on more than one occasion, been asked to lend my father money, five hundred dollars here and one thousand dollars there. I always got it back, but I had never suspected that my father had that sort of money. Crafty old devil.

The body was released after a few days, and after the funeral completed, we all went back to my father's house to set about putting things in order before going back to our respective homes.

That night, some of us went to have a meal before I went back to my unit. It was then that I brought up the slip of paper with one hundred thousand dollars on it and the percentages each one got.

"Mark that was 100 per cent, not one hundred thousand dollars," Stephan said.

"You're kidding," I said. "The piece of paper I gave you said one hundred thousand dollars. I remember that because I did not know that the old man had that sort of money."

I was told that as I was simply upset about my father's death, I probably wasn't seeing things too clearly, and I was mistaken. None of my protestations could change the situation and so I quietly gave up and went home.

Sometime later, I spoke to a local detective. I laid out the facts as I saw them: the happenings to my father, the wardrobe incident shortly after I was stopped from pursuing the superannuation money, and the sudden sickness that resulted in his death. To me, it did not add up.

The detective agreed with me and suggested that the superannuation money was the key. Whoever went after it clearly was the person who would become the number one suspect, in his opinion. I had a right to be suspicious based on the circumstances put before him.

All of this left me in a state of confusion. Clearly, I was being harassed and was under surveillance. This I had confirmed. But why was my father being harassed as well? Was there some commonality, or was this a totally separate issue? Was there nothing to do with my situation, or was there a link? What role did a million dollars play in this situation? Many hours contemplating my navel and pondering over the possibilities produced nothing. Questions came out of the woodwork at the speed of light. Answers came at the speed of a snail on crutches, always begging the question as to whether there was any connection between what was happening to me and what had happened to my father. What role did the superannuation play? Was this a causative factor?

Again, I took to pen and paper.

Was my father being harassed? Yes.

In what form? Phone calls in the early hours of the morning.

My father's name was called outside his bedroom window at odd hours at night.

The wardrobe was placed on the skirting board, enabling it to fall when my father went to place something on top of it—accident?

The request by my father, to pursue recovery of the superannuation money, and then after a visit from Stephan,

I was asked not to pursue it on the flimsy reason that it might jeopardise my father's pension.

Following another visit by Stephan, my father was admitted to hospital. This time he never came out.

Why were the only perishables destroyed were those cooked by Maryanne for my father? Other perishables were left in the refrigerator.

Why was the release of the body delayed so that a post-mortem could be completed? My father was sent to hospital by his doctor. He was supposed to be admitted urgently, according to the admittance staff. He was in the hospital for three weeks in the terminally ill ward. Why had they not determined the cause or reasons for his admittance and subsequent death?

Was I making something from connections that were not there?

I started to wonder if I had unconsciously walked under a string of ladders, broken a few mirrors, or had a dozen black cats walk before me. I considered all the possible things that I could have done to deserve what I was going through, and I kept asking the same questions. Was my imagination running away with me? Was I being suspicious over nothing?

Having been away from the family, apart from periodic visits, I was unaware of what had transpired in my absence. Because I had my own problems, I really did not pursue this to any degree.

Was there a connection between what had been happening to me and my father?

CHAPTER 17

After separating from my wife, I started learning martial arts and found that in addition to my physical condition improving dramatically, I also found a new confidence and awareness in my general outlook. One of the philosophical concepts that appealed more to me was, "Against softness, you use strength; against strength, you use softness." If someone goes to hit you, your instinct is to try to block it. My philosophy now is a subtle difference. Now I try to deflect it and then counterattack—one simple but very effective lesson. They have displayed their intent, and so now you are positioned to take whatever action you deem necessary. I applied this physically and psychologically and found it extremely useful when I started experiencing the funnies.

Slowly I got myself out of debt, and then I accumulated a few thousand dollars in the bank, in essence, getting back on my feet.

From experience in the divorce, I identified that part of the tactics used was to blacken the reputation of the other party and destroy him or her financially with a credit rating in tatters.

Accusations of paranoia, communistic, child molestation, and other titles were bestowed on the non-custodial parent. Denigration was standard fare. If I got to know someone going through a divorce, I often talked to the father, asking what accusations were being levelled at him. I confirmed that an adversarial situation was being maintained.

The flames of hatred were well and truly fanned. I believe that neither the custodial nor the non-custodial parent was fully aware of the reality of the situation. Both parties were being subjected to the treatment, embroiled in a well-oiled, multi-billion-dollar methodology.

At this stage, I had not really appreciated the length, breadth, and scope of the system. I was still trying to clarify the relationship between Theo and the divorce situation. My thinking was still subject to that area. My anger was directed at the legal profession and the methodology that they employed. It was many years later that I realised that they were a very important and essential part, but they were just another link in the supply chain.

After I left home, I did pursue equality in divorce, but the pressures of work, surviving, and living were a full-time operation. I slowly stopped doing anything proactive in that area. This did not stop the harassment. So why were they persevering? What objective could they have? Was there someone else as well?

I had firmly established that I was threatened. The cut car tyre was obviously a failed attempt to silence me. Now that it had failed, what would they resort to next to silence me from exposing whatever they thought I knew?

Why and how was the harassment continuing? I went through the potential natural causes and then some. On some nights, I would lie in bed awake, and I would hear the start of a phone ring or some other such noise.

If I was asleep, a phone ring would be just enough to wake me. I first became aware interstate, and then when I bought and moved into my father's house, it continued from that time. Was someone in the family involved? Was a combination of issues causing me difficulties? Was my father's inheritance a causative factor?

Was someone getting into my house and placing something in my bedroom? It had to be time activated to be triggered at a predetermined time.

I became aware of it when I was living alone interstate, and I was now living alone. Someone appeared to be entering my unit when I was not there. I would hear the noises, though never long enough to determine from which area they were coming. I knew that I had not imagined them.

The simplicity of gaining access to a house came home to me one occasion when I accidently locked myself out. I called the local locksmith and give him the address.

On his arrival, within minutes I was back inside. I paid the locksmith at the door and went inside. The question I often asked was "What if it was not my home that the locksmith had let me into?"

Whenever I sat down to watch TV in the evening, I would fall into a deep sleep. If a phone rang and I had to get up to answer it, it was as though I had been drugged. I staggered around for a while, totally unable to control my actions.

What I observed and thought was important was that one of my employees came over and was watching the TV whilst I went downstairs to get something. On my return, Greg was in the same situation, in a deep asleep. Thoughts of delusion and paranoia started slipping away. Something was going on. What I did know was it was not my imagination.

I initially put this down to being tired because I was constantly woken in the early hours of the morning. Then reasoned that a lot of people fell asleep in front of the TV so what was new?

I disregarded both events for a long time, dismissing them as quite natural. However, I did start asking questions as to what caused it, and I did some research into the potential causes. Again, there were a lot of questions but few answers.

Much later, I learnt about radio waves and their uses—or misuses, depending on the people involved.

I got to the stage where I would refer to my funnies and my phantom flatmate. On one occasion, when one of my favourite ties went missing, I left a note to my phantom flatmate to please return it and take another. This in fact happened.

These were some of the funnies, as I named them, and I slowly accepted that in addition to being under surveillance, I was being harassed. But who was doing it?

I felt that I really needed to add someone to the list of possibilities causing me grief. If I was going to be swimming in a sea of uncertainty, as they say, why not do it properly and add to the list of suspects?

I went back to the drawing board, relaxed, and listed some things I had now established as fact. Yes, it was confirmed I was under surveillance. Yes, I was being harassed. Yes, expenses were being incurred for me, designed to destroy my financial base and my credit rating. Cut my supply line so that I was broke, could not get credit, and had no money coming in. I would be destitute and destroyed. My ex-wife's words kept coming back to me.

In order of priority, I went through the potential reasons for the harassment.

The prime suspects initially were the solicitors. What had I done to arouse that? Why the solicitors? I had publicly declared that perhaps divorce should be taken out of the hands of the solicitors. Was I endangering their income stream? The field of divorce was a multi-million-dollar business. Much later, I found out that this was but the tip of the iceberg. I had expounded my theories on alternatives that would not establish an adversarial situation as the methodology during a divorce. I knew from the reaction I got from my own solicitor that I was not a popular person in his profession. Yes, I knew that they closed ranks and became protective.

A lot of the mail tampering was before and after I went on TV and radio, making comments and statements in the press. Yes, I knew that they organised private investigators to obtain evidence for divorce cases. Were the same tools being used again?

I let my mind run further. That accounted for the solicitors and their involvement. Where did Theo fit into the picture? I had now confirmed that he was involved. Suppose that he was making money from the solicitors? That they could be placed in a position whereby they were being asked for a percentage. I was a long time before I realised the other ramifications behind some in the profession.

I progressively started adding to the list as different situations occurred, but I thought I had it covered with the solicitors. Then Theo was added to the equation, so were the solicitors and Theo in tandem? That made sense; they had the money and the motive. How was I interfering with their income stream?

The thoughts I had put aside whilst driving over from interstate were never far from my mind, and now they kept coming back. Follow the money tree. If they were working together on the divorce situation, and the solicitors were making money out of that scenario, what was the tie-up with Theo?

I recalled a situation when I was working as a business development manager for a computer software company. Another BDM suggested to me that if I paid him 10 per cent of my commissions, he would ensure that I received plenty of leads. If I did not, my tenure at that company would be relatively short.

I quietly suggested to him to make like the pigeons and flock off, and we had a somewhat strained relationship from then on. I left the company to move to another venture shortly after. But this situation reminded me of the movie *The Godfather*, when a percentage of the takings was given out as protection money. Was it a coincidence?

To help sort out some of the confusion, I decided once more to commit words to paper.

The Car

Car tyres deflated to varying pressures after I had checked the accuracy of the inflation. Always a variation in tyre pressure. Amounts varies. Not natural, so how and when?

How? Slow leak in tyres—all four? Deflated manually? More recently: variation within 24–48 hours.

When? The time was between 2–4 a.m.

I experienced a very high number of punctures when I left my car on the street or not garaged.

Consumption increased appreciably from home base and returned to normal when away on holidays or at a friend's place for the weekend. I lost 20–25 per cent capability. Variable tyre pressure could account for some of the consumption.

Pause when commencing acceleration—slight hesitation adds to fuel consumption.

Loses acceleration capability, coupled with a pause when taking off from a stop.

Seat position varied frequently from the position I had left it the night before. I set my seat position for my size, height, and arm placement. It was often varied overnight. I put it down to a variety of reasons. This was noticed on the distance of the seat from the steering wheel, as well as the recline position on the back of the seat.

Body odour smells in the car when entering early in the morning. It was not every morning. I noticed similar smells in the flat on occasions.

Smell of acetate in car on occasions.

White spots on the steering wheel centrepiece, as if a spray was used. I had not used a spray

A couple of 9V batteries placed under the seat cover of my car. I did not put them there.

Something sounding like a tape rewinding when I switched off the motor. The cause was inexplicable; I had spoken to several mechanics.

Cost of repairs inflated—could be normal scam by mechanics but might not be. Mechanics trusted for years now appeared to run up expenses.

There was interference with my car's cooling system, causing overheating and a blown head gasket—immediately after a service.

A white spiral fitting under the front wheel arch-welded to the car frame, enamelled or plasticised white. Looked like an aerial. No mechanic or dealer could give me an explanation as to what it was for.

More recently, I would feel nauseous when driving to work or while behind the wheel. I didn't feel it when I switched off the air conditioner.

I was cautioned many moons ago to be cautious and not use the air conditioner in my car, because things could be added to it to cause the nausea. This was from an Italian friend. A couple of coincidental actions occurred when this friend appeared at places I was going to. At the time, I thought that it was too much of a coincidence. Was he another leg? He seemed to be aware of many things, and he did offer some advice that I considered useful.

The clock on dash in the car was not working for over two years. Then overnight, it started working again, showing within one minute of the time. Immediately after that, I started acting to trade it in.

The House

I was woken up every night between 2–2.30 a.m. This sometimes became variable and shifted to between 3.30–4 a.m.

Four hours of undisturbed sleep was generally the maximum. Conversely, I would become very sleepy at approximately the same times the following day, almost like I had been drugged. What was the relationship? How was this done?

I often went into a deep sleep in front of the TV. This was also noticed by others.

I would feel nauseous while working on the computer, mainly when connected to the Internet. It was not as much when I switched to using battery power only.

After I switched on my computer, I received a message tone on my mobile phone immediately afterwards.

When sitting in front of the television, I would often get a sharp pain emanating from the metal hip and knee joint replacements. I was told they acted as a conductor.

Noises waking me up, the phone ring cutting off partway through, and other noises that varied.

When I did a course with a private investigator, I was advised that this happened when someone was putting a tap on the phone. To connect, you let it ring twice. Before it rings the third time, you hang up. If you do not, a partial ring will be heard on the phone you are attempting to tap.

I frequently got a partial ring. Further, if you get an echo on the phone of your voice when you are talking, chances are that phone is tapped. I experienced both.

My clothes would disappear and then reappear when I was living alone.

I smelled body odour that was not mine upon returning from work.

Work

My work experience enabled me to prove myself as a successful salesperson. I was promoted to sales manager status and transferred interstate to lead a sales team. After two years, I was transferred to another state to set up the team there. I converted to computers and was offered a branch manager position. I was then employed in a general management position. In later years, I became involved with business software, specialising in what was deemed major accounts.

During this time, I was involved in many managerial training courses over a variety of areas. My training had always suggested that if a situation arose, I should look inwards first. After examining that side, then I could start looking at those around me.

The downside was that there was a tendency to become involved in useless introspection and disappear up a million tributaries that became confused and time-consuming until I got to the stage when irrefutable facts or situations surrounded me.

I was convinced that my phone was being tapped. I spoke to Telstra and arranged for a technician to visit my unit and examine the phone control panel. I was advised that there was nothing untoward happening at present, however someone had obviously been interfering with the connections because the way it was left, it was in a manner that no Telstra technician would leave it; their training forced them to higher standards. I asked for and received from Telstra a letter to this effect. It was another little cog in the wheel that dispelled my feelings on being delusional or paranoia.

It was this combination of events, together with the constant harassment and the costs associated, that caused me to enrol in a private investigator course. This was quite fascinating because I was taught how to tail people to their home and discover some explicit details about individuals. I learnt about the 'things' investigators did in the early hours of the morning. I learnt some of the traps of putting a phone tap on someone's phone and how to detect it.

I must have impressed the people at the course because I was offered a position as an insurance investigator when I finished. I declined because I did not feel that a change from computer software sales to an investigator was my calling.

CHAPTER 18

From what I could see and had now proven to myself, there was a beautiful mechanism in operation, and I had stumbled into it. The operation was as I'd thought initially, and I had worked it out whilst driving from interstate.

My theorising was accurate when the system comes into play. Expenses incurred through a divorce process are magnified and built upon. This must have a corresponding effect on the financial status of the warring parties. Eventually the assets need to be liquidated to bring about finalisation, which both parties want.

This then embraces another arm of the system. It also must happen as soon as possible to appease the banks for mortgages and sundry creditors.

I had proven this to myself with the sale of my property, but at that stage I was totally unaware of the length, breadth, and scope of the system. The fundamental reason why I was told to leave it alone was that I would be under surveillance.

This situation was definite and not imagined. I quietly went on investigating in background mode until progressively more pieces of the picture formed. This was much later.

In checking what I thought was happening on many occasions, I had talked to several people within the legal and banking structure and was advised that what I had stumbled into was correct, but I should be ultra-careful because the mechanism was a well-organised piece of machinery involving many people in high places from all walks of life.

Yes, it was operational here with very strong overseas connections.

Again, belief was a problem. The sheer magnitude amazed me. People going through divorce were victims, but comparatively speaking, they were small fry. So, what else was there?

The solicitors took all the flak for being unscrupulous in their dealings to win a case. This was regarded as part of the game. Were they incentivised? There was a tier behind the solicitors, and this was what I had stumbled on. This was what Theo was telling me that I was interfering in.

The solicitor's involvement was a vital cog but a comparatively small part.

The mechanism behind the scenes was brilliant. Initially I thought in the millions of dollars, but during my investigations, this was upgraded to billions of dollars, and probably trillions of dollars.

Whether to confuse or lead me astray, my most recent informant was that it was controlled by the CIA and Mossad, but because the latter was told to me by an Arabic informant, I simply filed it away, neither disbelieving nor believing. It went into the same bin as when I was constantly told to watch a movie called *Play Misty for Me.*

I was picking up little bits of information here, there, and everywhere and slowly putting it together; a picture was forming. One piece of the mystery was when I was told this had been in operation for about thirty years.

Well, there was a strange coincidence because that was the same time frame that I had initially been told by Theo that I would be found in the back of a burnt-out car, and that I was a marked man in New York.

I initially thought it was the European organisation and their operation. This was where I'd discovered it whilst going through my divorce.

The only possible explanation I could come up with was that there was a fear that I knew more than I did, and if it came to light, the entire mechanism would be in jeopardy.

If I was discredited and seen as an unreliable source, the accusations could be explained away.

Add to this that some time back, I was advised that Theo had long since died. Now it was not Theo. Had he left a legacy, and to whom?

Over the years, I gleaned that supreme excellence in a conflict situation was in breaking the adversary's resistance without fighting. What better way was there in achieving this than to employ the methodology of creating doubt, confusion, and disharmony? Confuse and mislead the thinking process, and create activity that surrounds the adversary, which forces his thoughts of paranoia.

This was precisely what I had experienced for a very long time, going back to Hertzberg. Good, old-fashioned FUD.

To go through these lengths, there must be something vast to protect, and I had stumbled into it. I did not consider myself an intellectual genius, but I did start putting little bits of information together and following my intuition.

During a divorce, for those who have not had this cleansing experience, all is laid bare. Your financial situation, your values within society every item about you, and your situations are written down and laid bare. Every semblance of your private life is exposed.

If animosity exists between you and your ex-partner—and frankly, if you are contemplating divorce, there must be some animosity—this than is fostered into an ideal position for this whole scenario to be turned into an adversarial situation between you and your ex-partner. If this is fostered by the participating parties, who is the winner from this arrangement, and how? Once established and achieved, then the direct relationship between you and your ex is irrevocably damaged.

Just suppose that this adversarial situation is fostered—the animosity, with each solicitor painting the adversary in the worst possible light. The father is painted as being a child molester, a bad father from many counts, and generally all things evil—whether fact or fiction, this becomes the perception. The mother's virtuosity remains somewhat unquestioned.

Herein lays a vast moneymaking machine controlled by the few to spread across several interrelated opportunities. Further, it goes right to the top of the chain, as high as you wish to go.

CHAPTER 19

I was frequently put in a situation when I had to give serious thought to the physical things that maybe I'd imagined. I was experiencing physical symptoms when I thought my head was in the clouds, falling asleep in front of the TV, aching joints, nausea when watching TV or on the computer (particularly when on the Internet), nausea when driving my car, falling asleep when driving my car, memory loss, and fuzzy thinking.

I was diagnosed with cancer, but fortunately it was in the early stages. Talking to doctors did little to diagnose the cause of the symptoms.

I was forced to employ the web to research. It was then that I discovered the symptoms I was experiencing appeared to be very like what was described as "radio wave sickness" or electromagnetic radiation. I found this to be a term used to describe a combination of electric and magnetic energy. This energy was transmitted from a source and radiated outwards in the form of waves.

Dependant on the power and length of the waves, they were classified into two main groups: extremely hazardous ionising, such as ultraviolet, x-rays, or gamma rays, and non-ionizing, which was visible light, infrared light, radio waves, and microwaves. Ionisation radiation was extremely toxic to humans. The hazardous effect on human health was apparent very quickly after exposure. Also, the artificial, non-ionising electromagnetic radiation, experienced from exposure to electronic and electrical devices, was also proven to be harmful and affected health in many ways. Even the consequences of exposure were not so immediate or obvious.

They found synthetic electromagnetic radiation to be emitted from cell phones, laptops, wireless routers, cell phone towers, and smart meters. There are ongoing, conflicting debates as to their influence on the human body and health.

As most people did, I used a mobile phone, a handset, a television, a microwave oven, and all the other appliances associated with modern life. These machines were powered by electricity and as such created and emitted electromagnetic radiation. Further, most electromagnetic fields interacted with each other to create even stronger, more hazardous effects. Based on this effect, EM waves were so densely populated that they became a health hazard.

I had two metal implants in my body. I was told that they acted as conductors for EMF radiation. I was experiencing a whole series of symptoms associated with EMF radiation side effects. Were these tools being used against me?

I was surrounded by these waves. Suppose I had the technology to use these tools against an adversary and increase the intensity of the harmful waves to bring about the desired results. These tools existed and enabled interference with electronics. This was evidenced by the American destroyer and the cruise ship that was reportedly rendered completely immovable by a Chinese aircraft.

Cell phones were regarded as one of the primary concerns, based on the intensity of the waves from a cell's internal antenna and its closeness to the head.

This was but one source; others mentioned included computers, computer pads, laptops, Wi-Fi routers and cordless technology, and kitchen and bathroom appliances. Combined, these devices increased the intensity of daily received radiation.

Microwave and radio waves are invisible and odourless, exposure is significant, and the consequences are often irreversible. Electromagnetic waves are known to overheat living cells; in addition, they influence the chemical structure of cells and non-thermally damage our DNA. Some of the side effects mentioned are headaches, sleep disorders, lower memory, and learning and attention capacity. It may be the cause of ADHD and autism in children.

Further, it reduces melatonin, which can lead to Alzheimer's or breast cancer. We as individuals have our own electrical circuitry within our bodies that is unique to us. It is our identifier.

Another article by Reinette Senum (April 2017) indicated that untested technology was being used in the United States that enabled sensors to be installed into everything—clothing, appliances, building material, cars, cosmetics, toys, computers, furniture, and so on. It turned our world into untested technology, further outlining and confirming my reading that everything and every object was connected to a wireless global network, allowing everything we do to be monitored and controlled and collected.

This is being achieved using a 5G network that uses new microwave, never-before-released millimetre wave frequencies (MMW). These waves are the fastest, shortest, highest intensity wavelengths within the microwave spectrum. Because the microwaves are short, varying in millimetre thickness, insects, plants, human skin, and eyes are especially vulnerable to them. The article further supports the argument that microwave radiation causes DNA breaks and cancers of the brain and heart.

This is not copied word for word, but it comes from the article https://medium.com/@reinettesenum/the-5g-network-what-you-dont-know-may-kill-you-f4361f46627f.)

The more I read, the more I was surprised at what I read, and the more it explained some of the inexplicable events to me.

The constant was that this was happening to me. There was nothing I could show to anyone else. I had no proof. I further discovered that radio wave sickness, as described on the web, listed some of the symptoms that I had experienced. Once more, the words of a song came to me "I've looked at life from both sides now, from up and down and still somehow, it's life's delusions I recall, I really don't know life at all."

Neurological: Headaches, dizziness, nausea, difficulty concentrating, memory loss, irritability, depression, anxiety, insomnia, fatigue, weakness, tremors, muscle spasms, numbness, tingling, altered reflexes, muscle and joint pain, leg/foot pain, flu-like symptoms, fever. More severe reactions can include seizures, paralysis, psychosis, and stroke.

Cardiac: Palpitations, arrhythmias, pain or pressure in the chest; low or high blood pressure; slow or fast heart rate, shortness of breath.

Respiratory: Sinusitis, bronchitis, pneumonia, asthma.

Dermatological: Skin rash, burning, itching, facial flushing.

Auditory: Chirping, buzzing, ringing in the ears, hearing loss.

Others: Digestive problems, abdominal problems, enlarged thyroid; testicular pain, sexual dysfunction. Dryness of lips, tongue, mouth, eyes, great thirst, dehydration, nosebleeds, internal bleeding, elevated blood sugar, immune system abnormalities, hair loss, pain in the teeth, deteriorating fillings, impaired sense of smell, light sensitivity.

(Source: "Radio Wave Packet" by Firstenberg 2001.)

I was always cautious of self-diagnosis, and it took a long time to accept that perhaps this was the cause of my symptoms. There was nowhere for me to go to have it checked or confirmed. I did identify many of my symptoms with those listed. Once more, I'd soak it up and get on with it.

When I spoke to my doctor, I explained, "Look, I am having these symptoms. I often get a skin rash, burning on my face, and itching. I feel thirsty frequently even though I drink a lot of water."

"How often?" he asked.

"Well, the best way to describe it is frequently and infrequently. Anytime I get on the computer or drive my car, I feel nauseous with a funny feeling in my stomach. I also get some strong pains running down my legs when sitting in front of the television."

"Are you worried about anything?"

"Yes, but this has been going on for a while."

"Well, everything looks well here. Do you have any of those feeling now?"

"No," I said. "I don't get them if I go away for the weekend or camping. I only seem to get them around the house or in the car."

He could not give me any answers. In fact, I got the impression he did not believe me.

On reflection, had I let myself be drawn into something I knew very little about, the only certainty was that I was out of my depth.

I was at the stage where I was willing to trade off what was left of my life to end the situation one way or another. Leaving them alone was not enough. They seemed to think that I knew more than I did—names, facts, documents. But all I knew was that there was something that wasn't above board, and billions were being ripped out of the community.

"You will be found in the back of a burnt-out car," I was told. In a very subtle manner, I was informed that I would be sent back to my wife with my face rearranged.

This took place in a coffee bar; it was not imagined. I was being harassed. Who was the guilty party or parties? My potentials including included Theo and the related financial institutions, banks, brokers, solicitors, and accountants.

My Ex-wife: "Play Misty for Me", my family. My father's estate was valued at over one million plus dollars. Did any of my relatives expedite my father's demise?

I had established that my father was being subjected to some degree of harassment common to both of us. How did this tie in with Theo? Did it at all? Was there another motivational factor that I was being drawn into that I was unaware of? Was there some someone in my circle whom I trusted and had access to my house, computers, and personal information, using it to his or her advantage?

Another in my inner circle, Martin, had just this ability. On checking his background, my enquiries revealed that this guy had a track record that I could only assume was dubious.

He was noted for forming relationships with women who were recently single and putting them in a situation whereby, under the cloak of assisting them, he positioned himself to take over their money and assets. His background as an accountant enabled him to present a successful façade.

Another friend, a professional accountant, advised me that he did not have the qualifications that Martin used to say he had.

In addition, he was somewhat secretive in his operations. He experienced "computer problems" that unfortunately destroyed all his client records and a series of similar incidents. This added to what I had been told about him, and it further added to my distrust and feelings of being on guard with him. No, I did not think everyone was against me—but someone was.

My reputation, credibility, and financial standing were being attacked as they had been interstate. Sleep disturbance, expenses created, and my supply line cut—it was all a rerun of what I had experienced before. The question was, how did they gain access into my house?

When I was living alone, it would have been easy. But I remarried and was often persuaded to go away for a weekend or a few days on some pretext. My wife was involved, but how? Was she coerced or threatened? Certainly, her behaviour at times wasn't consistent with what I knew her to be.

If she had been threatened, someone must have been using an indiscretion against her. Or was it more direct? "You have two sons. You wouldn't like anything to happen to them, would you?" Based on the threats made to me, I did not consider this beyond the level of the men with whom I was dealing.

Close relatives knew enough about computers to arrange the funnies. I was having my e-mail tracked, and my mail was not being delivered. They had access to the house and my computers. Today, this is very simple to achieve for someone with the right knowledge.

I was trained to identify behavioural incongruence. It was one of the many learning courses I had done to help me throughout my working career. I did find out that he had somewhat of a murky past. A few well-thought-out, well-placed questions at different times, and the answers given, caused me to believe quite strongly that there was something there.

It had started with my divorce. At that stage, the methodology was in its crudest form. Today, they are more sophisticated. Once more I had to marvel at the intricacies of the mechanism and the organisation.

I was living the life that whoever was monitoring had allowed me to live under their control and direction. They had violated my life because I was perceived as a potential threat or an opportunity.

I fell within the parameters of someone who could expose their operation or perhaps a source of revenue. It was outside of the scope that they thought was within the guidelines they had established.

Was what I had uncovered by accident and experience? Something was amiss. Or was there another reason that I had not considered?

On reflection, what had happened? I went through a divorce. Thousands did, so why was I so different? Therein lay the answer: I wasn't. And here lay the fundamental concept: when a couple separate and go through the process of dissolving their relationship, there is a high degree of distrust, animosity, and aggression towards each other. An adversarial situation is fostered further by some members within the legal profession. This is but one tool used by some.

There is generally an amount of property owned, either jointly or separately, by both that is accumulated prior to and during their relationship. Was acquiring this the primary objective? How was this achieved? There were many questions but few answers.

Initially, couples might agree amongst themselves that there is a fair and equitable division of property, as I and my wife did. But this was broken down by solicitors saying, "If you do not do as we say, we will not represent you."

This was what my wife had told me when I had questioned her as to why she had changed her mind regarding what we had arranged.

This was not put to me by my solicitor, and it was not the standard operating procedure for all solicitors. Mine only became hostile towards me after I went on TV to suggest that divorce be taken out of the hands of the legal profession.

I was attempting to interfere with their income stream, and that constituted a threat. The common denominator was not the divorce fees, even though they were quite extensive; that part was for the legal profession. The solicitors were part of the structural foundation, but as far as I could determine, they were the ringmasters. The circus owners controlled the acts.

Their role, though significant, was to use the tools within the system to paint the picture and provide the façade that justice appeared to be done.

The divorce situation today provides a steady growing supply of revenue and imposes the methodology that I have outlined. The revenue stream continues under the cloak of respectability and fairness.

CHAPTER 20

Thousands of people went through a divorce every week. Were they all being processed through the system the same way? Starting Children of Divorce enabled me to talk to many people who were in the same situation as I was, but not all people were being subjected to this process.

There appeared to be a group or cabal specialising in divorce that was employing this methodology. To this, add the cling-ons, who used this methodology to generate income from the situational position of individuals and trade on their misfortunes.

I was impressed by the moralistic standards they lived by and the methodology used to make money. I likened to their achieving the extraordinary heights of one with all the attributes to walk under a snake's belly holding up an umbrella.

It was several years before I realised that this process was not a personal one with me. I had personalised it by making an issue out of it and getting onto TV. I started to realise what Theo was trying to protect.

My belief was that the cut tyre and the threats confirmed that they were trying to hide something that they thought I knew about. The harassment was their attempts to find out just what information I had on whom—and to shut me up and not expose them and their operations.

This confirmed that it was not strictly legal, setting aside ethics. Further, there were several people in it and up to their necks who were afraid of what I knew. Initially, this was the only explanation I could establish as to why I was being harassed. It would explain why my flats were being entered. It explained why they were progressively damaging my reputation and credibility.

They had physically attempted to destroy me by cutting my tyre. This had failed, as had the concept that I had an accident. Therefore, if it could not be an accident, it had to be something that had the required result without drawing suspicion.

If they could destroy my credibility and standing. and if I then went on television and made claims, I would not be believed.

I had long decided that going onto a TV show was not going to be my preferred methodology. This I had done once before, expounding my theories on children of divorce. At that time, I had achieved my fifteen minutes of fame but little else.

In fact, the reverse had gone into play. I had alerted all and sundry on the other side that I was aware of some of the machinations. The result was that I had done more damage to myself than was done to whom I perceived as my adversaries, and I'd incurred their wrath.

Taking stock, I sat down to assess what I had achieved in relation to creating awareness as to what I perceived to be the situation. From the side of my adversaries, I had created FUD. They were afraid of what I knew about their operations, how much I knew, whether I could identify the players involved, and how much I could prove.

They did not know what names I knew, their involvement, and how much they would be incriminated.

I had been told on more than one occasion, "Mark, this goes right to the top." From what I could see, it did just that. It went right to the top, and they would have been afraid of exposure, with all the relevant consequences. I had also been told that it had involved a cast of thousands from many associated industries and professions.

During my divorce and the subsequent machinations, I had identified that some members of the legal profession were involved. Subsequently, I identified that this also embraced the banks—or more accurately, some staff within the banks. In turn, this would embrace the real estate profession. I became painfully aware of the accuracy of what I thought was the mechanism.

Behind all of this was the initially unknown factor. I must have put the fear of God into them to have them believing that I could jeopardise their operation.

"You are interfering in something you know nothing about."

For many long months and years, I had extreme difficulty accepting that I had stumbled into something that was well structured. But by whom? I always thought that I was drawing too long a bow, doubting myself. What had been put to me as factual by more than one person?

In fact, I was told that I was regarded as a whistle-blower. Eventually I decided that whether I was right, wrong, partially right, or whatever; I was in a no-win situation.

I had basically done nothing for many years and was still on the receiving end. My latest venture, building my units, saw me lapse into the same situation that I was in during my divorce. Or was this another facet of the operation in which I was becoming embroiled?

Although the divorce was very painful at the time, it did position me with a wealth of knowledge with my theorising as to how the machinery and the system worked. This put me into a situation whereby I was starting to predict events prior to happening in my current situation.

Talking about it was useless, so I only said what I must say.

Based on the decision that I was being hit whichever way I went; I spent a lot of time researching the various possibilities. I accepted that I was being harassed. This was taking the form of the previous methodology used on me: expenses being incurred, supply line cut, physical interference with my day-to-day experiences. I then came back to who had the greatest to gain by my failure.

Maintaining the surveillance and harassment over this period would require a lot of money and resources. Experience told me that it was private investigators physically causing the harassment. Who had the most to lose if what I was starting to accept and believe was made public? Who had the money to finance this over this period?

My ex-wife had the reason to bring something on, and this could be the root cause. She had connections with the European fraternity. Was she able to seek their assistance?

From what I knew, my relative had. Was this a factor to be considered?

My primary suspect was my old foe, Theo. Was there more than one? Had some teamed up? After identifying the possibilities of who, I ran the MAN test: which of the above had the money, authority, and need?

Based on all my tests, thoughts, deductions, and often a high degree of delusion, the number one suspect was Theo. To me, the rest were cling-ons.

Theo had all three. Money was not a problem; they had many millions in reserve and were making very large amounts. Paying for a private investigator to perpetuate the harassment was feasible and affordable.

Did they have the need? If they believed that I knew more and could prove that their activities were suspect, then if they could shut me up in a manner that looked natural, it would not be considered abnormal. Thousands die each day from these ailments, so why not me? It would look perfectly natural and normal.

"If I complain, accuse me of paranoia." Experience had taught me that people would believe this storyline rather than my unbelievable story. It was pure fantasy and, in a word, unbelievable.

The next alternative was a combination or combinations of some of these identities. My ex-wife had worked with the same European influence that I now believed was causing me difficulties, both before and after I had married and separated from her.

Although I did not believe that she had the money to perpetrate the harassment herself, in conjunction with her

European connections and any influence she could exert, that could have caused them to assist her whilst also helping them.

My relatives were involved within the financial structure or finance industry. As brokers, they had maintained contact with my ex-wife. Were they cling ons, having learnt how the operation worked and were now using the methodology to their own advantage?

Outside of the people I had identified, I could see no reason why someone would continue to harass me to this extent. The methodology, money, and motivational factors always brought me back to my primary suspect. I was always conscious that the primary suspect could be working in conjunction with or persuading other people to assist them. As I had experienced, threats to one's safety and family were not beyond the methodology being used by what I could only describe as cretins.

CHAPTER 21

I was rebuilding my life. I had married again. My new wife and I owned our house, and I had a little money in the bank. I did not have any superannuation, and so I had to do something to provide for my retirement.

To achieve this, I elected to knock down my house and build three villas as my retirement plan.

During the building of my units, I got the impression that I was being coerced to sell at least one of my units to a European friend. He had some Chinese customers and a shortage of property. He was of the same nationality I had identified previously. This was the same person from the same background who'd involved himself in my life. But knowing him and the methodology he displayed, he alerted me to the possibility that maybe the people in the legal profession were involved, whereby a percentage of their earnings were being paid to the organisers of the system from the fees they collected.

This operation had to include staff within the banking sector. This would embrace the finance sector and allied businesses to include accountants, mortgage brokers, insurance companies, real estate agents, and all associated areas. Was I getting carried away? Was I playing with myself? The questions always remained.

Initially, my thinking in relation to the system was centred on the broken marriage and divorce scenario. But a lot of situational factors came home to me during my development project. Plans were drawn and quotes obtained to complete my costing projections, based on advice given to me.

In addition, I built in an on-cost factor of 25 per cent. After being provided with a building quote of eight hundred fifty thousand dollars and eight to twelve months for completion, I then provided an additional 25 per cent, or one hundred eighty to two hundred thousand dollars, as a provision for building that was quoted as a little over one million dollars. This was to complete the building within eight to twelve months.

I applied for a loan for one million one hundred thousand dollars. I was confident that this, together with the reserve that I held, covered for all contingencies.

The accountant I was using was also a finance broker and had collected the figures from me. He arranged a loan for one million dollars within a few days. This was regarded as a "low docs" loan and was granted almost immediately without the requirement to complete my company paperwork and documents, as required by another bank. I was delighted. I was also told that I could obtain additional funds later if I required them.

I was not to find out, nor was I told, that the bank officer in the loan department had assumed that I would be using my reserve fund of two hundred fifty thousand dollars to finance the building project. This only came out months later, and it only surfaced when I submitted bills for payment and was advised that the bills submitted were not actually for building expenses. I would be required to pay these myself from my reserve fund.

This was one of several mistakes I made. I assumed that the building costs would have included the architects' and engineers' fees, as well as all associated fees directly connected with the building project. I had to pay these costs from my reserve account.

In addition to this, the building was being delayed for a variety of reasons, such as late payments to the builder. The building was running very much beyond promised due date. The building invoices submitted by the builder were not being paid within the allocated time frames, and the builder was becoming somewhat agitated.

Several costs increased. The quote to connect the water tanks to the required drainage went from approximately two thousand dollars to over ten thousand dollars. Oh, you want air conditioning in all the units. Another twenty thousand dollars.

The cost of building went from eight hundred fifty thousand dollars to over one million one hundred fifty thousand dollars. I was told by many that this was standard fare. All of this appeared to be a standard operational process and was in line with what was considered normal business practice. I was the dumbo for not knowing that this was standard fare, but it was what I was progressively identifying as the system.

I had to do something quickly, and so I again approached the broker. The broker, in his wisdom, could arrange additional finance for me at 4–5 per cent per month interest or 9 per cent per annum. The builder had some contacts with which he could arrange finance.

Between us, we went back to the bank, financing the original loan. That bank wanted to have a valuation done, and this was duly arranged. The valuer came at the appointed time and gave an indication of $1.6 million, appreciably below the valuation I had arranged independently.

It was at this juncture that I realised that again there were many coincidences. The officer in the bank, responsible for granting and controlling the loan, and the valuer who valued the property to enable a loan increase were of the same nationality as Theo. In addition, a colleague I met through my normal work environment became somewhat friendly and wanted to play a role in the development; he too was also of the same nationality. All of this was a coincidence, of course. I could not really fathom what he was doing at that stage, or that I was being harassed. A local spending a lot of time maintaining contact with me was also of the same nationality.

It was then that I noticed that the name of the person controlling the loan within the bank somehow had his name removed from all documentation and correspondence on my computer. He was also of the same nationality.

I started to wonder what I had stumbled into. It must be much bigger than I'd realised, and all the thoughts of million-dollar scams were not fictional. It explained the harassment, the amount of money spent on harassment, the interference in my life, what I perceived as the gradual demolition of my integrity, the spread of the notions of paranoia, and all the things I experienced. Once more I was lost in the wild and scared as a child.

CHAPTER 22

I t was at this point that I made the decision to commence fighting back. A large part of my life had been destroyed. I was forced to leave my daughters and friends when I became a victim to the system. The system was in operation then, and if anything, it was going much stronger and more sophisticated now.

My losses outweighed my gains, and my life was being controlled by somebody. Whom was I fighting? Now I was prepared to trade what was left of my life in order to get this whole thing aired and made public. I realised that I was a very small minnow in a very big pond. As I had always said and believed, I should follow the money tree.

Back to square one. All my troubles seemed to start when I was going through the divorce. During this period, I appeared to be going through the normal divorce process. Therein lay the truth. How normal was the divorce process, and was it beautiful machinery for generating income from unsuspecting clientele? Who was controlling who?

Again, this appeared to be normal practice or standard fare. Communication and the relationship between me and my ex-wife could only be regarded as non-existent and hostile; this is encouraged and fostered by some.

As my wife had said on more than one occasion, "If I do not do what they tell me to do, they will not represent me." This appeared to be fostered by some members of the legal profession, so any amicable arrangements between the two separating parties were not an option. Why?

I was questioning more and more the motivation, concluding that there had to be more to it. Now the picture was becoming clearer each day.

To in any way imply that all solicitors were all a bunch of crooks and ripping off unsuspecting clients would be totally incorrect and erroneous. This was made clear to me by a couple of very senior solicitors from large organisations who guided me whilst telling me my theorising was correct—but I should be careful and leave it alone.

These aspects of the chain were perfectly normal and could be expensive, but they could be totally above board and within the system for dealing with the warring factions within a divorce when they were charged with the task of achieving the best outcome for their clients.

They were also the ones best positioned to identify and form the complete picture of the warring parties. Herein lay one of the major identification points of the individual parties to identify their qualification as candidates for the system.

Not all were part of and using the methodology, but who was and was not was harder to determine. There were many qualifying factors and parameters; these were identified by those using the system during normal divorce processes. At this juncture, normal process objectives were established.

System identifiers were established; one of these was the ability to pay: what asset did they have that could form part of the separation process? How could they be separated from their assets? Exceptions to the process were identified and established, enabling the action process to be followed.

Utilisation of computers to assist the control of these functions could dramatically simplify the control process. Alerts could be used to advise the respective parties and identify when action was required once designated parameters were identified.

Through this identification process, effective business intelligence rules and tools could be used to monitor and control the process.

Each person's situation could be parameterised with control points. Exceptions were identified and controlled with alerts to notify the controllers when or what action was required—or more important, when they fell within the parameters and were eligible for the system to become operational.

Salient information was sent to the staff lending authority when a lending authority was involved: a divorce process was in operation; stop recovery procedures.

This was normal business practice when you have employed a legal representative to look after and achieve what is deemed to be in your best interests.

Assume that there is a family home involved with a mortgage and one or two cars, some money in the bank, and other assets. Many people were living from day to day.

Another scenario was that the husband is the recipient of a salary or may be self-employed; in today's terms salary, he could be making more than eighty to one hundred thousand dollars. For the wife, it was if she was also making in excess of sixty thousand dollars.

They could also be reliant on the income from the husband if the wife was not working.

All of this forms a part of your net worth, and if children are involved, the percentage chances of the husband being granted custody of the children by the courts is distinctly less than the wife being granted custody. This is normally the situation, whereby the wife is granted custody. She is painted as the person best equipped to look after the children.

To achieve this, the husband is often painted badly or is accused of other unsavoury acts against his children, implying he should not be granted custody and will only have visitation rights, in many cases under supervision.

CHAPTER 23

Intertwined with this situation, I was dealing with some commonalities with my father's harassment. This created difficulty reconciling with any of Theo's activities. However, there were some common denominators.

What I had established was that on each occasion, that one relative, Stephan, visited my father. After his leaving, some mishap would befall my father. The last one was his needing to go into hospital, from which he never came out.

This was the same relative who demonstrated to me his ability to span many areas when I was in his office, and he caused my mother to lose her job.

At that time, I really could not fathom what his reasons were. It was only years after that the penny dropped at to his attempting to show me the power he possessed. At that time, the subtlety of his message eluded me.

Another common denominator was sleep disturbance, with my father being woken in the early hours of the morning by a telephone call. The time was consistent with when I was woken up at the time I was told that private investigators did these naughty things.

This relative combination of husband, wife, and son had persuaded my father to not attempt to recover his superannuation, which at that time amounted to more than one million dollars.

My mind went back to the time when I was interstate for a few days for a business efficiency fair, and I contacted Stephan's son. I was invited out for dinner.

The meeting was very pleasant, with the small talk that one goes through during the meal, touching on a variety of topics in relation to the family.

After dinner, we sat down in front of television and chatted. Shortly after we sat down, I went into a very deep sleep for over one hour.

When I woke up, I felt very heavy and was staggering around for a while, causing my relative to suggest that he take me back to the motel.

At the time, I put this episode down to my being overtired. After relaxing for the first night that week, this sort of thing was quite common. As Stephan's son was now a medical student, I did not give it a second thought for some time. A long time afterwards, another common denominator fell into place.

He stopped studying medicine and went into his father's business, where he acquired an in-depth knowledge of computers. He had since changed his occupation and had become a mortgage broker.

I gleaned these bits of information from family, but so what?

As time went by, I tried to establish the attributes essential to causing my father and me harassment, and some of these factors came into play. Sleep disturbance was one. The method used to achieve this was another

I established that Stephan's son had been in contact with my ex-wife. Further, I gleaned at some stage that this relative's son was considered strange by some of his own family. Slowly more of the pieces started falling into place.

The possibility of a million-dollar payout was a decided incentive for Stephan to discourage my father from pursuing his superannuation. Knowing that my father was not in the best of health, could he have sped up my father's demise? Was I chasing rainbows? Always I had to consider: was my imagination running riot, was I clutching at straws, was I losing it?

It was after this that I decided I must throw one of the last suspects onto the list: my ex-wife. Much later, I discovered that she had told a couple of people that she had hated me and wished I would have an accident on the way home from work. That confirmed my best interests were away from her.

Things in relation to her became increasingly suspect, and when people kept telling me that I should watch a movie called *Play Misty for Me*, I often wondered what they knew that I did not.

I became aware that she had been in contact with Stephan's son, and there had been more than one discussion within that area. Was there a link?

A question always lingered. She had worked for and with people with the same nationality as Theo. She had a very close relationship with one of his employees.

What had I stumbled into that had caused the number one suspect, Theo, to start working me over? He was my strongest suspect. I took my thoughts and notions to the federal police. They referred me to the police interstate. After I laid out the story, the common request was, "What proof do you have?" I could prove nothing concrete, and on reflection, it sounded like a beautiful story that I had concocted. As a result, I achieved nothing from going to the local police or ASIC.

Some of this was because I was not sure in my own mind what was fact, deduction, and all things in between. Most important, there was no concrete evidence; or as they put it, it was very interesting but did not substantiate my story.

Now facing the cold hard facts of reality, I could not prove anything was amiss. I had a lot of thoughts, theories, and deductions but few facts. Over the period of my life, I knew what I had been through. I knew it was not fiction. I had not imagined the threat from Theo, and I had seen and had to pay for a new tyre because mine had been slashed.

I had now made my feelings known to the police, and so I was on their radar. Whatever was to happen to me had to look like something very natural—hence the radio wave interference.

I had been quietly studying people and their behavioural habits to realise that behind me, something was going on. People could hide many things when dealing with people, but there were some things they couldn't easily hide in relation to the way they acted, the actions they took, the way they behaved or, and the position of their eyes while talking.

So once more, you are in this situation, Charlie. You cannot explain it to have people believe you when you are up to your neck in uncertainty yourself. You have no facts that you can show and have someone feel touch and see. So, you have nothing.

This led me to my philosophic approach that no matter who you are or what you think about anything, people are going to come out of the woodwork to tell you are a bloody idiot for holding that opinion, and you should be doing it their way. After years of being caught up and led astray in my younger years, I learnt that you really need to work on the you factor—what you want and think of yourself.

You decide what you want, what standards you want to keep, and what you want for your life. Set aside the Shouldabaters and Mustabaters. I had determined a long time ago that these people came out to tell you that you are an absolute fool for doing things the way you are, and you should or must do it their way.

Shouldabaters are people I closely liken to Mustabaters. They tell you what you must and mustn't do and how you should do it the way they think you should it. In my experience, both become and trigger self-hate.

CHAPTER 24

I sat down once more and took a step back. Whatever Theo and his crew thought, they had spent a fortune on their FUD. What I was jeopardising? The only explanation for the constant harassment was their attempt to shut me up.

I knew facts as I understood them but could not show them to people; I had nothing. So just what did I have? Speculation, deduction, imagination, and personal experiences.

Take that to the police, and it is not considered proof. Talk to friends about it, and they immediately start making preparation for your admittance to the funny farm.

What neither of the divorcing parties is conscious of is that they are being processed through a very sophisticated system whereby they are designed to suffer the cost of divorce with all its entrapments whilst being preoccupied with the animosity that adversarial situations generate. This is common practice by some within the legal profession. Fortunately, there are many solicitors within the legal profession who are aware of this methodology and warn against it where applicable, as I was by a leading solicitor.

The structure embraces many tiers within the profession and, where applicable, the relevant associated industries.

I was now on full alert thanks to Theo. I had identified that legal fees, though substantial, were the thin end of the wedge and were part of the payback to the legal profession for being part of the grand scheme.

Money was made by the cling-ons. So, from a divorce point of view, you are put in a situation whereby you must sell your assets as quickly as possible so that you can pay your accumulated debts and get on with your life. You are correctly guided into the thoughts of your well-being and the future well-being of your children.

I cannot recall having met a man who does not regard the welfare of his children as paramount within this process. Once more, we have a right side, left side brain function conflict. Logic and emotion—who controls what, and in what way?

One example of this was when a father whose income stream was destroyed by the process was required to pay maintenance of one thousand eight hundred dollars per month. Alternatively, he was then asked to sign over his share of the property as settlement to his wife in lieu of the maintenance payment. Like me, he was put into a situation whereby he had to sell his property to achieve settlement. This was done as a quick sale situation, producing well below market value, and it was sold using a nominee sale process. This is a common practice and is one of the methodologies used.

CHAPTER 25

Keeping these aspects in mind, I again looked at some other methodology that could be employed to deter me and dissuade me from continuing my investigations. One was consistent with some of the many aspects to which I had been subjected.

On one of my research sessions, I came across information highlighting radio wave activity. Technology is available to invade your privacy, twenty-four seven, three sixty-five. Further, it can be used to harass a person and cause severe discomfort or even death in a variety of ways. Was I being subjected to this?

My foray into the effects of radio wave technology opened my eyes to many things. If I was correct, it explained many of the symptoms I was experiencing. Always the questions remained. *Well, boyo, are you really experiencing these things, or is it your imagination playing tricks with you again?*

You saw the cut tyre on your car. You saw the clock that had not worked for over two years now be within a minute of correct time. There are a host of other situations that you saw, felt, smelt, and touched, both in your unit and in your car. Get real—you have a problem. Look at the facts.

In attempting to sort fact from fiction and avoid delusion and advanced stages of paranoia, I researched many areas.

In an article by Donna Fisher in February 2017 (Nexus, April–May 2017), she stated that "everyone is affected by electromagnetic fields (EMF) from babies to manufacturers to those who do all they can to prevent policy change" Donna highlighted that

> all living beings, are dynamic, coherent electrical systems reliant on bioelectricity for life's most basic metabolic processes. Electrical rhythms in our brain can be influenced and altered by external signals-altered informational content which cab swamp natural electromagnetic cues and result in dysregulation and desynchronisation of normal biological rhythms that direct growth, development, metabolism to maintain health. EMF alters the electrical signalling which directs the chemical messaging system in the brain. As the brain directs all body processes, physical and mental disorders result from EMF exposure.
>
> Our body and brain operate on inherent, natural, subtle signals, beneficial information which is dependent on exquisitely timed internal cues and life

prompting with information from nature. It is critical to life that this relationship remains intact. EMF is a human-made signal that contains information.

Peak millisecond radiation bursts have an impact on our body at the cellular level. Our cells provide energy and safeguard DNA. The overall activity of a living creature depends on the total activity of all the individual cells: If your cells function poorly, then tissues and organs will become comprised. Biological systems of the heart, brain and gut are dependent on the cooperative actions of cells.[1]

Further, she states,

current guidelines/safety limits adopted by most western countries, were developed by industry, based on out-off- date research on thermal effects, i.e.—The short-term effects, instantaneous-the heating of tissues as in a microwave oven. If it does not heat you it does not hurt, you.
This is being proven increasingly to be not true. As she goes on to say that wireless radiation should be re-classified as a human carcinogen.

---

[1] https://www.nexusmagazine.com/articles/doc_view/351-nexus -volume-24-no-3-april-may-2017

> The largest salivary gland-is located near the ear where mobile phones are typically held during use.

Within this article, a statement by Dr Milham points out that there has been a gradual increase in the mortality rates of cancer, cardiovascular disease, diabetes and suicide; the so-called diseases of civilisation.[2]

The World Health Organisation, in "Electromagnetic Fields and Public Health: Electromagnetic Hypersensitivity", states that several health problems related to EMF exposure. These include redness, tingling and burning sensations as well as fatigue, tiredness, concentration difficulties, dizziness, nausea, heart palpitations and digestive disorders.

All of this was a very strange coincidence. The symptoms were consistent with what I had been experiencing, and progressively there was more evidence that I was not going crazy.

Another article by Reinette Senum, dated April 2017 (Nexus, June–July 2017), states very clearly that a US National Toxicology Program study deemed that microwave radiation causes DNA breaks and cancers of the brain and heart. This was caused by the new 5G rollout stating unprecedented numbers of new millimetre-wave radiation frequencies are about to be released on the public. This is despite the, 2G, 3G, and 4G technology proving to be toxic to our health.

The ability to link the symptoms I was experiencing with the symptoms I was reading about and could associate

---

[2] http://www.who.int/peh-emf/publications/facts/fs296/en/

with, together with the behavioural characteristics of the cling-ons, was putting the pieces of the jigsaw together. Increasingly I asked myself, "If I could be identified, and all my movements and activities tracked and monitored by government bodies for metadata purposes, then why was it not possible for this information, in the wrong hands, to be used against me to satisfy their objectives in this manner? I had been told that I was identified as a whistle-blower.

I now had a logical answer for why I was feeling how I did, and once more I pondered the question that if something subtle was required to shut me up, what better methodology was there? I could die from a heart attack, a stroke, cancer, or a variety of other ailments that looked perfectly normal, particularly in today's environment and at my age.

My experiences had taught me many very interesting life lessons. Some I had wished that I did not need to learn. My skills for separating fact from fiction were becoming increasingly tuned for many years, and as such I felt I had become quite adept at separating the two, particularly in this environment. Further, I was much more capable of distinguishing the doubters around me and setting aside non-productive or interfering trains of thought introduced to me by well-intentioned friends.

I had established that couples going through a divorce were ideal prospects for the system to be put into play. I had firmly established that both were designed to lose because the ex was now firmly on the other side. An adversarial situation was established so that divorcing parties were not talking to each other. But they were just one source of revenue and exploitation.

We had started Children of Divorce to gain greater equality for the non-custodial parent, only to find that winning the case was paramount; usually at severe financial loss to both parents. We had also established that for this to work as it did, it had to involve more than those within legal profession. They were pivotal, but there were other players. The operational philosophy of the profession included judges involved in divorce situations. The various state governments were all supportive of and working with the system.

More important, the members of the profession who were involved within and using the system to feather their own nests were only one of the identifying feeders, or as I called them, cling-ons.

I did not consider myself an intellectual genius, but I kicked myself for being as thick as a brick for not seeing the light of day previously. Finally, pennies started dropping, and the picture started to become clearer to me.

During all this time, one of the major fatalities was the condition of the children. The combination of the animosity between the parents, and the situation of having a father once a fortnight, often disrupted the financial status, resulting in the ongoing effect of feeling guilty for bringing all this about. Rejection and a host of other feelings, both imagined and real, had a devastating, long-term effect on children's mental well-being.

If you closely examine this structure today, together with the number of marriage and relationship breakdowns affected in this manner, you must wonder just what role we play to bring about a situation that affects the mental health and stability of our children. It's something we are causing daily.

CHAPTER 26

What will end the situation, return peace, and create the ability to start a new life? A quick settlement that will meet the agreed status and situation. To achieve this, wherever applicable, liquidation of mutual assets and division of property is commenced. If the assets include property, a real estate agent is attuned to the situation with a direct interest in the methodology employed. Speed is the essence to enable outstanding creditors to be satisfied, one being the bank or financial institution. Peace and normalcy is supposed to return. One can only ask, "What is normal?"

The property may not realise its true market value. A tame buyer is positioned to purchase the property. This has been shown to happen time and again. After the warring parties are out of the way, the property may then be put back on the market to realise its true value.

It took me a long time to establish that this chain was operated by many staff within the loans department of the banks. The banks were the heart of the system.

The operation, from advice given to me, showed it went right to the top. I had personal experience with and had witnessed the working model myself on two occasions.

The operation working with divorcing couples alone was very lucrative. But I was not going through a divorce when I went through a development project and discovered that there were a lot of common denominators within the methodology.

The same characteristics, and coincidently the same nationality influence, worked the same methodology many years later.

Was it again my imagination, stupidity, and the variety of other reasons I used to initially think it was? I had firmly established that I was a victim of the operation. I also identified that I was not alone. There were thousands of others that were going through a divorce. They had a young family and a mortgage, and they were battling to survive.

Who is responsible for this situation? Are all fathers who are accused of mistreating their children guilty? Do all fathers completely lose sanity and start doing deplorable things to their children, or is this a methodology employed by some to achieve an objective? As I had discovered, this situation is real. The methodologies employed are generating a lot of money. I had thought in terms of millions, and I was corrected to billions by senior staff within the financial sector.

The divorce business alone, although very lucrative, is not the only area. Today, as it has been for a long time, couples scrape and save to buy their homes. It's the average young couple's dream. As life progresses, children are born, their expense to income ratio changes, and things become harder.

There are situational factors beyond their control, such as interest rate increases. Loan variations and additional expenses push them to and beyond their limit. The number of loan defaults increases daily.

Consider this, as we have seen in Australia there has been a very large depreciation of property values. From 12.15% to 20%. Now suppose you invested in property to boast your superannuation scheme or position you as you got older. You accepted an interest only loan to finance your investment. On completion, say your property is valued at $3,000,000. Now we devalue it by 15%. Because that is what we are set to believe that properties, over the past few months, have devalued and, dependant on the area, from 12.5% - 20%. You have just lost $450,000. With your property now valued at $2,550,000. You are now placed in a position whereby you must sell. You're an absolute fool, how did you let this happen?

This is happening in Australia today. Costing people billions. Thousands are affected. Take this methodology overseas. Where it came from. How many billions are involved? The figures are beyond me. But look I am delusional, paranoid. This could not be collusion could it. Could it?

Just stop and think. Can this be a construed situation where people are intentionally placed into a default situation? If yes, by whom? Remember that banks are but a tool, one link in the chain. Ask yourself, who has the right to devalue property to this degree? What investment parameters issued by one financial institution and taken up by the financial sector, suddenly determine that we need to correct an inflated market. Who inflated the market, how? Have we set aside the rules of supply and demand, are we manoeuvring a situation?

This was the system that I identified within the divorce area, spreading over to other areas. We blame the banks, the pressures of life, and the stupidity of the people; this is but part of the system in operation.

They are put in a position whereby they must sell or close their businesses because they are no longer able to service their loans. The bank forecloses. If this situation was brought about solely by the bad management of the individuals, this truly would be one of life's disasters. If the situation was brought about by their bad management or lack of planning, this would be soul destroying. But just suppose that this situation and some people could be manoeuvred into a situation. How advantageous would this be to people working within the banks, their associates, and all their relevant contacts to exploit the situation to their own advantage? Look at this as the supply chain. The banks are but one vital element, but they are not the controllers.

The issues that affect the victims from all aspects are devastating, and we see them happening every day. They are labelled in many ways: credit rating, psychological effects, strain on the relationship, and a variety of other factors that they are seen and portrayed to have brought this onto themselves.

Just stop and think. Can this be a construed situation where people are put into a default situation? If yes, by who? Remember that banks are but a tool, another link in the chain.

It is prudent management for banks and other lending bodies to monitor and manage their exposure for a loan that they have financed.

The loan departments are responsible this because they are supposed to protect their exposure. Today there, are many computerised tools available to assist them to do this. A relatively standard accounting system, tailored for the banking industry, assists them to control the loan ledger, interest payments, delinquency, and the normal attributes required to be maintained for loan, credit, and management control.

Imagine now that they have the business intelligence tools to establish parameters to determine risk factor, delinquency probability, and other associated parameters. Now imagine that the loan and credit department staff can direct a what-if question at the customer's accounts to enable them to compile risk analysis based on the parameters they have established. From this, they can determine the vulnerability of each client. With a large client base, they can set clients' vulnerability base to fall within the parameters that they have deemed relevant, isolated, or reported on.

Computers do an excellent job computerising, and so now we have a list of loan customers that fit the parameters—customers who can and are put on watch.

Now imaging you are in the loan department of a bank, and you have been advised that divorces proceedings are underway in relation to one of your customers. That account could be frozen. The account is earmarked for the reasons given.

The account may or may not be regarded as a delinquent account at this stage, but now after advice from the solicitors, it is marked accordingly. As a member of the team in the loan department of the bank, you are advised that one of your creditors could default because of impending circumstances.

This customer joins a list of vulnerable clients in front of you. Part of your job is to recover the money for the bank.

I again refer to my building project. I submitted invoices for payment. Some were not paid by the bank because they were deemed to not be building costs. They were consultant fees for correct drainage, tree preservation, and drainage fees escalated from a quotation of two thousand dollars to more than eleven thousand dollars. Additional costs such as this are escalated dramatically, all appearing to be quite legitimate. The bank advises that these were not within the scope of the building and as such were to be paid from my reserve, not the bank loan.

The builder's invoices were delayed and not paid on time, creating friction between me and the builder. Costs were escalated beyond the parameters I initially established. I was reaching the stage where I was running past the bank loan as well as my reserve.

An approach to the broker to have the loan increased produced some offerings at ridiculous interest rates from private lenders. The bank would not increase the loan value.

The bank started making noises about recovery of the loan, and it had valued the property to me at about 75 per cent of what I knew market value to be—a difference of about six hundred thousand dollars. When I approached another mortgage broker from a different company, the loan was agreed to with another bank, and the valuation was closer to what I thought the property was worth.

Now I could complete my project and continue living. If the other bank had been allowed to proceed along the path that it had planned, I would have been financially ruined. They would have picked up property that they had valued at $1.6 million. Correct alternative valuations were for $2.25 million plus—a difference of six hundred thousand dollars.

I had clearly identified that the methodology in play during my divorce process was the same used during my building project. Now I had established that this was a common methodology used by some of the staff within the banks, together with their associated cling-ons.

I had also established that a simple but brilliant methodology was in play during my divorce as well as more refined processes. I had seen ample evidence that this same methodology could be applied throughout the industry. Staff in the banking sector had confirmed my belief as accurate.

I used to visit a small country town that was primarily a centre for local farming. The township contained a small mixed business that included a garage and a restaurant. It was ideally used for the locals to pick up some supplies, as well as a meeting place where the locals had a drink and joined friends and neighbours for a chat. Across the road was a hotel that also provided food. It became obvious to me that both venues had fallen victim to the system. Now, not only were they not operating, but one had become a storage area for a couple of caravans and expensive cars. Previous discussions with the owners made it abundantly clear that they were victims of the system.

Where does it stop? Does it ever stop? Why? How many combinations make up the millions and billions that I had been told about?

I asked myself, "What if banks were not the main players in the operation but merely acting as a tool or go-between?" As always, I questioned my theory, and a million doubts and questions came out of the woodwork. Was my imagination at work again? But the question kept coming back. For this to work, where was the money coming from to be distributed?

If I likened banks to a distribution business engaged in distributing and selling a product, I'd term that a distributer. Consider that banks are acting on behalf of a manufacturing company. They may not manufacture a product themselves, but they distribute the product on behalf of the manufacturer or supplier.

Liken the banks to a similar situation. The difference is that they distribute and use money to make money. It's like a business with products supplied to them. Money is supplied to the banks, and they distribute it. Again, it's like a business distributing products from several suppliers. So, a bank is ideally situated to distribute from several sources.

If this is operational here, it must be operational overseas as well because comparatively speaking, we are relatively small compared to America, Canada, London, China, Europe, the Middle East, and a host of other countries. What had I got myself into?

Every step brought doubt and further questions. If this was as large as it appeared, then Theo could not have been alone—again, he was part of a cabal.

Australia, where I first became aware of this, is comparatively well off from a financial standpoint. The interest rates were higher than overseas countries, and the standard of living was supposedly higher than Europe, causing it to be called the lucky country. As such, money was being brought into Australia because it provided a better, safer return on investment than overseas countries. Could Australia be used as a launderer?

CHAPTER 27

nvestigation based on this theme led me to an article by a Patrick Henningsen, an investigative reporter based in Omaha, Nebraska. It supported my thoughts in relation to what I thought was going on. From the information provided by Patrick, he established that there were really four banks in Australia. These banks brought both private and public money into Australia. They were primarily supplied by four international banks. The four banks controlled and directed the financial sector—the subsidiary banks, insurance companies, and mortgage brokers.

This view was supported by an article I had read entitled "Bankster Paradise: How a Small Elite Rig the Game of High Finance", written by Patrick Henningsen. Patrick had illustrated it as follows.

The tree looks at the ownership of Australian banks. The companies at the top of the tree are the top four shareholders for all the banks in the following level. The percentage shown is the total ownership these four companies have of that bank.

After reading these articles, I was not sure if I was confused or afraid. Was I reading too much into the situation?

Or too little? Once more, confusion reigned. I was not on solid ground, which annoyed me. I had a lot of speculation, conjecture, assumptions, and all things in between.

But of one thing I was certain: if Theo was involved in this type of operation, then I could understand why I had been given the warning that I had. Further, if this was the case, how was he going to shut me up? More and more, it became obvious to me that my connecting with state, federal police, and ASIC might have been one of the best moves I could have made.

Unwittingly, I had negated the direct action of Theo's connections such as the cut tyre, the threat of being sent back to my wife with my face rearranged and being found in the back of a burnt-out car.

Were these banks being used as a laundry for overseas money coming into Australia? Was this what Theo was concerned about? What was his involvement with this situation?

Private and public money was being brought into Australia. How was this money being used in Australia, what was this source, was this being laundered by the banks, and for whom? Was the money laundering associated with the areas that I had stumbled into? Questions poured out.

Staff within the banks appeared to be involved, and from what I was told, it went right to the top. But again, I had nothing concrete and no definite proof.

When looking at the banking structure in Australia, I was intrigued. Again, the how, what, where, and why came pouring out of me with questions aplenty, but tying it together was a totally different story. I had spent hours trying to work out the questions in relation to Children of Divorce and trying to get the structure changed. Was there a connection with Theo and the banking or financial system?

Clearly there had to be one, otherwise why was I being harassed as I was? What if Theo was using the banks to launder money? This had been talked about before in many areas. The banks were the ideal vehicle to achieve this. I was putting pieces in the jigsaw and increasingly being told that my theorising was correct, but proof escaped my theories.

Looking at the banking structure in Australia, there were four primary banks. These four owned varying percentages of the other banking and financial institutions. But how did it all fit together? Conversely, the overseas banks had a percentage share of the Australian banks. What was Theo doing that that fitted into this structure? Was this a part of the structure that he was involved in. What was the connectivity with the people getting divorced. Where they just part of the supply chain? The questions went on.

The Australian Banking Structure

Private Money/Public Money: Illuminate. Overseas Banks Others?

Overseas Banks NAB, HSBC, JP Morgan, Citibank

Australian Banks; Percentage ownership by overseas banks in Australian banks listed: Westpac, National Bank, Commonwealth Bank, ANZ Bank

CHAPTER 28

I had now established that Theo's involvement with couples going through a divorce served as part of his customer or supply chain. I had identified that he was only part of it and not the only source of the supply chain; it was a building project.

This same methodology was imposed on young couples trying to put house and home together, small businesses, and people struggling to put a business together. Generally, the bank financed it. Then consider any business area, building companies, normal trading companies, importers, and distributors, and where did it stop?

For this to work as effectively as it did, it had to involve and embrace many people from all walks who acted as feeders. With the divorce sector, there was the legal profession; this would embrace people within the banks. Because property was involved, it must then include the real estate profession and accountants.

Advice would be required: "What should I do?" Logically, that would come from an accountant. Could they be involved? Can they make money from the system if their advice supported the activities imposed on clients? Of course, one must be insured for a variety of reasons. Was the insurance companies' part of the link?

Were people allowed to insure with someone other than the company that the loan company suggested? Did the banks have any connection with the insurance companies? Add to this the people I termed as cling-ons—those who had become aware of the operational capability of the system, knew how it worked, and adapted it to satisfy their own purposes.

This operation reminded me very much of when I was a young boy and watched western movies whereby the small rancher was struggling to maintain his property. His next door neighbour, a much bigger ranch owner, wanted his property, and so he would poison his cattle, destroy his water supply, and do a variety of other evil deeds to destroy the rancher and persuade him to sell or leave. This of course would be at a price advantageous to the big ranch owner.

The small ranch owner was often a woman, leaving the door open for the hero to come to her rescue. The hero was often portrayed by the likes of John Wayne, Roy Rodgers, Joel McCrea, or some other equally heroic personality.

In this case, I was not a woman. When I really wanted assistance, or someone to discuss my perception of the situation, I was ridiculed. Getting someone to believe me and take me seriously was an exercise in futility. But the game plan was the same: position players in a weaker position that enabled you to take over their possessions at your price, not theirs.

To operate something of this nature and embrace the billions of dollars involved, where was the funding coming from? The common denominator was the banks. Banks had a seemingly endless source of supply that they used to fund their normal banking operations.

In an article by Patrick Henningsen, his opening paragraph talked about a complete vacuum of ethics, fuelled by a complete and unprecedented orgy of cash and institutional credit. Welcome to the world of the modern banker. They were funded by public and private money. Where was the private money coming from? Further research brought me to an article by a Russian in relation to the financial sector.

Recently, the *Guardian* featured a remarkable account in "Global Banks Are the Financial Services Wing of the Drug Cartels" by Ed Vulliamy. This article stated quite clearly that the conclusions formed suggest that the financial services play but a secondary role in the tandem. Their role was in money laundering rather than playing a key role in the drug business. The article depicted an alliance between drug cartels and the banks. Further, it quoted an expert on organised crime, Misha Gleny. It described a syndicate: "the cartel is a holding company, an agglomeration of small, flexible mafia groups", boasting a considerable extent of decentralisation. This agreement spanned several countries such as the United States, the UK, and others.

Allowing the whitewashing of the cash flows generated by drug sales meant revenue investment in various sectors of the economy ("Strategic Culture Foundation" by Valentin

Katasonov, June 2012, https://www.strategic-culture.org/news/2012/10/06/global-drug-mafia-and-the-banks-an-introduction-to-the-subject.html).

The *Daily Telegraph* on 16 Tuesday February 2016 featured "Down Underworld in Grip Of Mafia" by Charles Miranda. Outlined the extent of Italian drug money coming into Australia. One must assume that overseas companies were active in Australia. It had been stated that Australia was one of the major channels for drugs being shipped to the United States from Afghanistan, and that the Lebanese and Afghans were constantly at war in Australia, fighting for control. Once more there was a series of unrelated facts, but establishing connectivity was another situation.

Discretion was necessary and caused me to back away from this scene entirely.

Theo was an Australian, and he was of European decent. He had influence within some members of the legal profession. Through Theo, I had identified that they were involved with the divorce industry, where I was attempting to change the process. This had caused a warning from Theo. Increasingly: I was starting to see connectivity between what he was doing and what he was involved in. What had I stumbled into?

My theory, if correct, was that they used money to source legitimate enterprises. You obtain money they have deposited within the banking or financial structure—private money. For any reason, you are forced to default; you may be assisted to do this. The bank goes into recovery mode to protect their assets and repossess within their network. The mystical people in the cloud have now laundered their money. They legitimately have acquired assets quite openly and honestly within the system. It's a brilliant mechanism and was only part of the supply chain.

The System: The Supply Chain in Australia

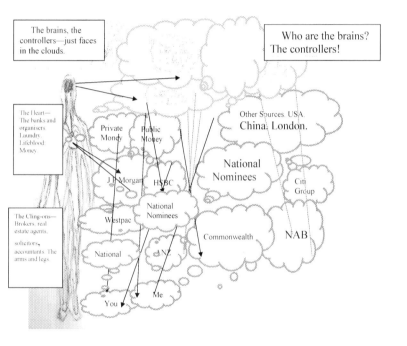

The brains, the controllers—just faces in the clouds.

Who are the brains? The controllers!

The Heart—The banks and organisers. Laundry. Lifeblood. Money.

Private Money

Public Money

Other Sources. USA. China. London.

National Nominees

J P Morgan

HSBC

National Nominees

Citi Group

The Cling-ons—Brokers. real estate agents.

solicitors, accountants. The arms and legs.

Westpac

Commonwealth

NAB

National

ANZ

You

Me

CHAPTER 29

I had now become attuned to sitting down and thinking through what I thought was going on to get some degree of understanding and sanity back into my life. I accepted that I really didn't know life at all.

I believed I had established what Theo was doing and how I had become entangled in a mysterious web that had become all-consuming and taken over my life? It required a conscious effort daily to set aside thoughts in relation to this situation and concentrate on living my life and returning to normalcy. I was always asking, "What is normalcy?"

In a divorce situation, to talk in terms of character assassination would be an understatement. The concept of establishing an adversarial situation between two divorcing parties is common practice. When couples were in this state, the cling-ons moved in to pick up the spoils.

I had tried to change this situation to enable fathers to establish a better relationship with their children, and I'd suffered the consequences. This had been thwarted in a variety of ways. Several senior people within the legal profession had told me that I was correct in my views, but

I should be very careful about my personal safety. Some things were best left alone.

All of this told me that a lot more people were aware of the system and could not or would not do anything about it. Was it deemed to be the system to be used by all relevant parties and condoned by controlling bodies in order to achieve their objectives, and where applicable, they turned a blind eye to the subsystems in operation? Or once more, was it the FUD factor? I had been threatened by Theo in just this area.

This was a trillion-dollar business, and yes, it was very much a commercial operation. As with any commercial operation, the intent was to generate revenue. I was advised that this concept provided large amounts of revenue. The people involved were far-reaching from the controllers to the operators to the feeders, both in Australia and overseas.

CHAPTER 30

On reflection, many things fell into place in a variety of ways, with some causing more confusion than clarity. One of those was that whilst visiting Stephan in his office, Stephan picked up the phone and rang my mother's employer to advise him of her true age and his exposure for employing her if something went wrong. My mother lost her job shortly afterwards. His explanation was totally beyond my understanding at the time, and it was something I never even thought about apart from thinking it was a strange episode.

In hindsight, was my relation trying to show me something? This was the same relative who was later responsible for receiving money after my father's death. He was responsible for getting my father to stop me pursuing this money. Also, I was interstate on a conference and was suffering the same symptoms, falling into a deep sleep in front of the television.

As I had established, many people fell asleep watching TV. But how many were awake one minute and in a deep sleep the next? Further, when I got up, unplugged the TV, and took out the electrical wall plug and aerial connection, the feelings of sleepiness went away, as well as the burning sensation I used to get in my ears and the itchy feeling I got under my skin and around my joints, knees, elbows, and hips.

They used to say someone was thinking of you when you got the burning sensation. I called it many things, but the feeling was quite intense.

Was it a coincidence? Was there a connection? It took me a long time to establish that the burning sensation was possibly a by-product of electromagnetic radiation, and it took much longer to confirm to any degree of certainty that EMF was a causative factor.

Stephan used to be in contact with my ex-wife. He was a mortgage broker, as was his father. This was fast appearing as a common denominator. What I had discovered with my father's death was that I was increasingly establishing common ground. My ex-wife had promised to destroy me. Was there a tie?

Some incidents and occurrences that I had not even taken into consideration at that stage could have been the result of the connection between my ex-wife and Stephan's son.

Add to this my father's estate situation, and was this a causative factor? Was I really going crazy and ready for admission to the funny farm? It was a question I often asked myself.

Both for my father and me, the aerial under the wheel arch of my car, the phone calls in the middle of the night, and the other strange incidences—these I saw and felt. All the other occurrences over the period confirmed that

I was not losing it, so now it was a case of confirming who and why.

Clearly someone wanted revenge, or something was driving it. Was it fear? My credibility and in a subtle way my character was being destroyed. At the same time, they had attempted to create FUD within me as far back as Hertzberg, creating feelings of paranoia.

I always asked myself what they were afraid of. What did they think I knew? More important, what did they fear I would expose? I was always asking myself what I was supposed to know.

The Theo connection was a definite. I had proven to myself that there was involvement from that direction on both instances, my divorce and when I was building my units. They had unintentionally exposed many circumstances that enabled me to fill in the blanks.

My ex-wife related to what I used to consider being a European don in the state where we used to live. It was not the same one who threatened me, but one who I determined to be influential in many ways with many connections of the same European background. All of this proved to me that perhaps I was on the receiving end in many ways. If I went to the police, ASIC, or any other body, the first question asked was, "What proof do you have?" To explain to them what had happened, when, and how was an exercise in futility. What I had was not considered proof. So once more, I went back to my thoughts, resources, and judgement.

So, what had I established? People going through a divorce provided for a brilliant mechanism that was a source of revenue for various players: the solicitors involved and the associated services they employed. The solicitors acted as a front for the other activities. Their activities were directed at the court processes and satisfied the essential legal processes. Within this arena, they had to ensure that all the correct legal requirements were being adhered to for their clients.

I was constantly reminded to not confuse legality with morality. Something could be deemed perfectly legal but was in fact a subtle interpretation of the law. There was a difference.

Based on this, I had seen and been a victim of this manipulation. Divorcees played the game whilst searching for peace and a degree of normalcy, with the perception that they could now rebuild their lives.

Peace was the final objective, and rationality was a blurred myth. The division of property was the final episode. The custodial parent was to be maintained, and the father or non-custodial parent was to maintain the children. This was logical and required by law.

One of these causalities of divorce was the mortgage because now the assets needed to be liquidated. Either the bank moved to sell the property to recover their exposure, or this was arranged in conjunction with the banks.

The surrounding situational factors ensured that this must be expedited to enable the banks and other creditors to protect their exposure. Herein lay another of the key controlling factors.

This situation was controlled by and monitored by the loans department within banks. This was understandable because they were seen to be responsible for the outstanding or delinquent debts. The recovery process or mechanism came into play, and they were responsible to reduce their exposure. Alternatively, arrangements were made with the solicitors to stall the situation until an appropriate time. All of this was strictly legal and was an essential business practice to recover the monies owed to them.

From this point on, things became a little tainted, and the aspects of morality and legality again become blurred. Speed was the essence. Was it possible that the persons responsible, that staff within the loan department, assigned the sale to a trusted real estate agent that they had worked with before and had established an amiable and financially beneficial working relationship? Again, it appeared quite logical and legal, seemingly following good business practice.

A valuation was completed that appeared to be a normal process. But the valuer was assigned by the bank or possibly the person in the loans department. Was the valuation in the client's best interest, the bank's, or the person within the loan department controlling the situation?

Was it possible that the valuer, sent by the bank, undervalued the property to satisfy other interests? He was seen to be an independent valuer, but was he really? Enter the real estate agent. Again, was he part of the chain? He set to it with a will, conscious of the fact that speed was essential.

A buyer was identified, and the sale value might be discounted to enable the bank to quickly recover the money.

Could the buyer be part of the chain? In my case, after my divorce, the sale of my property was completed via a nominee. From what I could ascertain later, at best it was at about 60 per cent of market value.

On the surface, it was done to achieve the best result for all concerned parties. Peace could now return, settlement could be completed, and the divorce situation could be finalised. As I believed, I could now get on and rebuild my life.

At one stage, they used to stop when they had cleaned you out during a divorce process. Now they just whistle on through and sign you up for the next few years. The children must be maintained, their livelihood must be protected, and all things must be done to ensure their ongoing safety. Again, it seems logical and reasonable.

This process appears to be maintained by what is perceived to be the pillars of our society; barristers, solicitors, and accountants appear to be involved. Are they benefitting from this process? For this to operate as effectively as it did, it had to involve some specific people within the government departments who were benefitting from or aware of it.

I had discovered, after talking to some very senior solicitors, that not all played the game this way. Those I spoke to were aware of what I was talking about. As always, I was cautioned to be careful because there were many wheels within wheels, and where significant sums of money were involved, many factors came into play.

As everyone is aware, divorce is a very traumatic experience for all associated parties in which the elements of FUD thrive. Confusion reigns supreme, emotions run high with all parties, and clear thinking is a causality. Working on this aspect can this be used to the advantage of those inclined and experienced in the methodologies available to gain advantage and make money from it.

As I had discovered and experienced, there were many using this methodology to gain their objectives at the expense of the warring parties within a divorce.

A high degree of lip service is paid as to what is in the best interests of the children. On the surface, the system is seen to be doing just that. They attempt to make all the financial arrangements to ensure that the children are maintained by the respective fathers. The parents are manoeuvred into a situation that in many ways is deemed to be in their best interests. But is it? How many couples are financially destroyed? Is this in the best interests of the children? Yet "justice" appears to have been done. This is the system employed by many. How can one confirm this? Talk to friends going through a divorce. You decide whether the methodologies I have outlines are being employed.

This is a well-oiled piece of machinery that embraces many different structures to be recognised as the system.

Finding and identifying the many elements involved within the system took a long time and was an ongoing process. Trying to not involve those close to me was another exercise.

I had established what was going on every day in normal life. Divorced couples were one section, or feeders, in the supply chain. It was not until I embarked on a building project that I noticed the mechanism come into play again. The mechanism had now become standard practice, and not only for the people going through a divorce. As I had experienced, the operational philosophy had been picked up by what I called the cling-ons. My initial experience was with the European contingent. I now established that it was more widespread. Or was my vivid imagination running rampant again? What proof did I have?

CHAPTER 31

had experienced some unbelievable situations during my harassment process, causing me many hours of FUD. Initially I did not believe, but then I was in a situation when I did not have any alternative but to believe. It took me a long time to wake up to what Theo was trying to protect. It took me even longer to realise that this was only the tip of the iceberg.

Take up the same methodology, and the world is your oyster. You have sections of the public totally exposed to all the refined trappings of the few who organised and exploited many.

When I embarked on a building project, I required a building loan from a bank. I obtained all relevant estimates for building, allowed for cost overruns, and commenced operations. During this period of building, I came to thank the European people who placed me through the learning curve of my divorce experiences, because of the similarities within the process to which I was again being subjected.

The same European descent structured and operated via the loan department within the bank. From square one, they were the same origin. When I went to investigate and attempt to correct the situation, and I went for refinancing, a lot of names I was dealing with from the first bank disappeared from my computer. Again, as Doug would say, funny! A lot of other computer records disappeared.

Was it a common situation with all banks, or just the one with which I was dealing? Which bank was involved? No, it wasn't just that one. That was not the one that nabbed me; it was one of the others.

Progressively, I discovered it was not one bank. Once more, as I saw it, all roads led to Rome. But why be prejudicial? Why not Athens, Beijing, Beirut, Moscow, London, or New York?

Australia has established a reputation for being a very clean country, and laundering money was but one of the cleaning processes that had been established.

How was this being achieved? One method I was told about was that there were many people of who frequented the casinos; they went there and lost large amounts of money. To me, going in there to lose a million dollars a night was a large sum of money.

But as I was told, in so doing they would have deposited and laundered some twelve to fifteen million dollars. To launder twelve to fifteen million at a cost of one million was less than a 10 per cent commission. One person doing that two or three times a week showed a quick return for some substantial sums of money.

I was but a babe in the woods as far as money laundering went. This was just one arm of the operation, and I soon decided that I was better off not knowing all the ramifications of this methodology; I was better staying out of it.

Further, from what I could see, there was no connection between what I had been told about this aspect of laundering and Theo's operations. Therefore, discretion being the better part, I elected to stay that way. I was in enough trouble with what I was forced to learn about factors I knew nothing about.

If the same methodology used on me was used generally, I was starting to see where the billions of dollars they were talking about came into play. The process was the same as my experience when going through the divorce.

All of this was standard and prudent financial lending practice. Banks were a lending authority, and they had lent billions of dollars to the public, businesses, and a variety of other institutions. It was their right to ensure that their investment was protected and that they took essential steps for them to protect or recover their investment and reduce their exposure. As such, they provided the perfect vehicle.

From a loan application, a client's full credit history is before the bank officer—his income, expenditure, assets, and liabilities. It identifies the history of the customer. Payment difficulty, arrears, missed payments—this identifies his vulnerability, or risk factor.

A borrower may be having difficulty meeting his commitments. Payments are late or missed. Now, provided with the information that a prospective client is within the parameters and now has satisfied the requirements to qualify for the system, they can trigger their recovery procedure.

Within this process, costs are escalated beyond the debtors' ability to pay. A 0.5 per cent interest rate increase would create a whole new list of prospects for the system. This was what enabled me to identify the banks as the heart of the system.

In my project, I was out of money, and the builder could not give me more time and wanted his money. The bank that financed the building loan was making noises about foreclosing. They would not lend me any further money to enable me to complete my project. The mortgage broker was making noises about loans of private money at over 9 per cent interest, as was the builder. I was fortunate enough to be referred to another mortgage broker working with a different bank.

If the bank in question had been able to foreclose on my loan, they would have made a profit of over six hundred thousand dollars very quickly. But as I had established, it was staff within the loan department of the banks controlling the issue. Were senior management involved? They would have to be.

I was starting to wake up to what the true situation was, and now I was convinced that Theo was involved with this type of operation.

I was relatively small fry, but remembering that from little acorns mighty oaks grow, I pursued my beliefs. On talking to another contact, I was advised that a builder had embarked on a building project to build six hundred units. He had been subjected to the same methodology and experienced the same result. Imagine the financial situation and the value of six hundred units! Yes, I was small fry.

Whomever I talked to: I was advised that this was the mechanism. Friends in the banking system, people in business, accountants—they all said the same thing. All cited the same figures and talked in billions of dollars. How and why was this allowed to continue? And without proof, how does one stop it?

This was why my life was being interfered with. Someone wanted my assets and thought that they were more entitled to them than I was. If I let it come about, as in a divorce situation, the result was that both parties lose everything. One blamed the other, and animosity lingered for years.

The money tree sheds its petals in a variety of different areas, dependant of the hierarchical status.

I sat and pondered. If all of this was open and above board, why had my computer records been altered? Why had names been removed? How was this done?

This I knew was relatively easy for anyone with a modicum of knowledge within the right areas. My knowledge was with business software. I had long ago left the bits and bytes, the negative and positive side.

I was still involved enough to know in which areas to go looking to identify the methodologies employed—and more important, start looking at the ways and means to slow the onslaught.

CHAPTER 32

Whenever I drove my car, I felt nauseas. Driving a car to go and meet clients and potential clients was part of my livelihood. I also noticed that when I stopped my car and switched the motor off, there was a noise very like a tape in a tape recorder winding back, coming from under the dashboard. No mechanic I talked to was able to explain the source of noise to me.

If I switched off the air-conditioner, the feelings of nausea diminished. If I opened the windows of the car and switched off the radio, the feelings of nausea abated further.

I would go to my car in the morning and often find that the position of my seat had changed overnight. On occasions, body odour lingered in my car. On a couple of instances, it appeared that a white spray had been used on something, and some residue was on the steering column of the car. A cut on the brake handle was inexplicable.

The car was locked in a garage overnight, so how was this happening? Earlier at a previous address where I'd lived, whilst I was having my house built, I would suffer a very high number of punctures—nails in the tyres and equally annoying incidences. Other costs were being incurred for me in relation to the car: a blown head gasket straight after servicing, only to be told that I should have checked the oil levels.

On reflection, the incidence of cost being incurred for me and by my car seemed to have gone on for an eternity. There were two incidences of damage being done whilst the car was parked, one whilst I was living interstate and one locally. On both instances, repair work was required that had me inconvenienced for quite some time.

When I sat and thought through the strange incidences that I had encountered, I had no alternative but to think that someone was interfering with my car. I initially put this down to the solicitors and because I had talked on TV about taking divorce out of the hands of the legal profession.

I had established that there was some form of interference with my physical well-being. After many hours of research and assessing, I had determined quite definitely that I was being subjected to electromagnetic radiation.

Many years ago, I was advised about the use of EMF within the air conditioning unit in my car as the tools used to achieve this. At that time, I had dismissed it as nonsense. Now I was confident that it was not nonsense. Furthermore, it was done in a manner that made it look natural and normal.

I had come close to falling asleep at the wheel—easily put down to driver fatigue. Nausea could be put down to travel sickness. There was cost elevation for repairs, such as someone reversing into me causing damage. On the return of my car from the panel beater, the spare wheel was not there, taken out and not replaced whilst being repaired.

Increasingly, I had established that some forms of electromagnetic radiation were dangerous. Placing a smart phone directly to one's ear is now shown to be the cause of brain damage, cancer, and other similar issues. This situation is magnified for children, who are much more susceptible than adults.

Today we incessantly use computers, notebooks, smart phones, and tablets. Combined with Wi-Fi, these items are proving to be the causative factors for cancer, blood pressure, brain damage, and a list of other ailments that are increasingly becoming common.

I had experienced severe pain in one of my knee joints. This ultimately led to a left leg knee replacement operation. Some twelve months prior to this, I was diagnosed with a small cancer in the bowel, which was removed; fortunately, it was in the early stages. I was now being monitored, confident that it was under control. Seven months later, I experienced severe pain in his right hip. I was advised that this was relatively common because the knee operation was probably one of the causative factors for the hip to be affected. Therefore, I had my hip replaced. I had every confidence in my surgeon; he had done many operations before, on all areas, and came highly recommended to me. The hip operation never seemed to settle down and after popping on more than one occasion. The surgeon decided to do the operation again three months after the first operation.

On the way back to the orthopaedic surgeon's office, after the surgery and four days after my release from hospital from the hip surgery, I experienced chest restrictions. On advising the orthopaedic surgeon of the situation, I was immediately admitted to hospital again for fear a blood clot had formed after the hip operation.

I spent the next ten days in hospital whilst they attempted to ascertain the cause of the internal bleeding and the chest restrictions. The cause of the internal bleeding was never determined. I was told that the cause of the chest restrictions was the result of arterial blockages on the arteries going into the heart. Immediate attention was required.

During the previous twelve months, I had endured severe joint pain, and because of this I had two operations on the same hip and a knee joint replaced. I subsequently had to have stents inserted into two arteries. In addition, a small cancer was removed from my colon.

When I went back to review the occurrences, I noticed that many of the symptoms could be caused by radio waves and cell phone emissions.

Further, I was advised by an authority that the materials used for knee and hip replacement would act as a conductor for the radio waves, magnifying the effect of the EMF radiation because the inserts were metal and acted as conductors.

I sat down and considered the other situations that I had been exposed to, confident now that what I had theorised and established on EMF was correct. I now cast my mind to the aspects at home.

Falling asleep in front of television, I went out like a light. When I was on the phone at home, I noticed a burning sensation in my ears. I also got this when I was working on the computer.

In addition, I would get feelings of nausea and extreme discomfort if I used battery power on my computer instead of being plugged into the mains. The feeling of nausea, burning in his ears, and discomfort dissipated appreciably.

Making a connection between these situations and EMF took me a long time—too long. I had pondered the questions on there being any connection between the occurrences that I had experienced. I was put on alert when I was contacted by an acquaintance—the same one who had suggested to me in a very subtle way that I would be sent back to my wife with my face rearranged; he was of the same European descent.

He wanted to set me up with a device that would enable me to view and record any TV channel quickly. I was not a big TV viewer and declined the offer.

Further, he also suggested to me that some of the problems I was experiencing with my replacement surgery were quite common, adding that I should join a group with the objective of suing orthopaedic surgeons because there was a history of this type of situation whereby patients had experienced ongoing difficulties.

This intrigued me because only a few months earlier, this same person was looking for the name of my surgeon because he was having problems with his knees and felt that he may have to visit a surgeon. In good faith, I gave him the name of my surgeon only to be told later that my surgeon was a clot. Some weeks later, he said that I should join in the group that was suing orthopaedic surgeons.

The same person was trying to get me to sell one of my investment properties soon after completion. This was not in my plans, but again, it was friendly persuasion. Tony was somewhat forceful because he had Chinese buyers lined up.

When I considered that Tony was also involved in real estate development and wanted me to use his talents for my development property, it strongly confirmed to me that Tony was not as he appeared on the surface.

I had wondered on this before, but as always, I put Tony on a "watch and see" mode. I started studying his behavioural patterns. I arranged meetings for coffee and fed him in a variety of different ways. After examining and thinking about the series of events, I categorised him as either tied with the initial connection or a cling-on working with the initial connection.

In many ways, I had to thank him because he brought to light an idea that I had not considered and had overlooked. It tied in with Theo.

Relating back to what Theo was doing; I was concentrating on what I thought was attaining the assets from divorcing couples. Tony had thrown another possibility into the arena. The assets were just part of it. If Theo had arranged to take a percentage of the fees that were involved from the participating solicitors, here was another revenue stream that I had not even considered.

If he was taking just 10 per cent of the fees from the participating solicitors, and the average fee was fifty to seventy-five thousand dollars, that represented up to ten thousand dollars per divorcee, or up to twenty thousand dollars per couple. More than one thousand couples per annum were divorced across Australia, but based on that figure, it amounted to approximately up to twenty million dollars. Was it my imagination again?

If I was correct, this was in addition to the money being generated by the sale or acquisition of the assets—again, a comparatively small return. But it was an avenue that I had not considered before, and I now placed Tony amongst the people using the system to his own advantage at the expense of me and people like me.

As always, behavioural characteristics told a story, but the story was told to me. I had seen and confirmed many things that I knew were being activated. But it was I who had seen it, and I could not show it to someone else so that they could see, touch, or feel anything. I could not say that I had definite proof of anything untoward. Tony had demonstrated to me the underlying methodology. I was supposed to make available to Tony a percentage of the development as a payment for my being allowed to keep the balance. This was the payoff. I'd sell him one of the units at a preferential price, and I would be allowed to keep the other two. Back to *The Godfather*.

CHAPTER 33

was told by more than one person that I was regarded as a whistle-blower. As such I was being treated accordingly. I identified that the staff in the loan department of the banks were the lynchpin, one of the major control points.

I had established this initially from Theo's actions, which triggered my quietly investigating what I thought was the situational factors controlling the operation.

Later, incidents put the picture together. The name of the officer from the bank I was dealing with disappeared from my computer, along with all my soft copy records.

The combination of events the threats, the harassment, and the warnings confirmed that there was something much deeper going on. I had stumbled into a very small part of it. The organisers who put the whole thing together were the Theos of the operation.

The banks were critical but were only part of the operation. The organisation was spread through to include real estate companies, solicitors, accountants, and staff within the relevant government bodies.

My initial exposure was through the European connections, but as I progressively discovered, the Middle Eastern influence was heavily involved, as was the Oriental sector.

I never ceased to wonder how I had got myself into this situation whereby I initially was trying to get a better situation for myself and other non-custodial parents. This got me onto TV to clarify that all fathers were not animals whose interests were no longer for their children. I believed that fathers deserved a fairer position.

But on consideration, many factors emerged. Not all solicitors worked the system. Many had the same feelings towards it that I did. Likewise, not all staff in the banks were involved. Defining who was and wasn't was the challenge.

This was initially the trigger that alerted me to the system. From this, I realised that from a non-custodial parent position bringing significant change was a utopian dream.

I was to accept that this was the system as dictated by all ruling bodies, and my punitive efforts were not going to let anything, but superficial changes happen. Furthermore, the divorce system was a well-oiled, remarkable piece of machinery designed to generate income. The divorce machinations were but the window.

I accepted that I was too small to change the system. It required more than I had. All I could hope for was to show it for what it is. More important, I wanted to expose the methodology in play to extract billions of dollars from an unsuspecting public.

As I continued my investigation, I was astounded as to how this was being achieved, and how exposed we were to the various elements in play.

Couples divorcing are the ideal candidates for the system to be put into operation, but this is just one source of supply.

CHAPTER 34

Today we live in an era whereby machines such as TVs, computers, smart phones, and microwave ovens are all part of everyday life, both at work and at home. This exposes us to the effects of electromagnetic radiation, a form of energy that is transmitted from the source and travels outwards in the form of waves.

These are classified into two main groups: ionizing, such as ultraviolet, x-rays, and gamma rays, which are regarded as extremely hazardous, and non-ionizing, such as radio waves and visible light. It is this type of radiation that is extremely toxic to human beings.

Today, life would be extremely difficult without the use of this technology, but these machines are powered by electricity, and because of this, they create electromagnetic fields that emit electromagnetic radiation.

Non-ionizing, microwaves, and radio waves have been identified as the cause of serious illnesses. The nature of the microwave is such that it takes time for the development of any illnesses to be identified.

Further, electromagnetic fields interact with each other, creating more hazardous effects. We are living in an environment densely populated with EM waves, each with varying degrees of hazardous effects on human beings.

I developed what I thought were normal and natural symptoms that I was unsure of. That started me on the exploration as to what could be causing this situation. Initially I was diagnosed with a small cancer; fortunately, it was in the early stages, leaving me with the thought that I must now always be conscious of that situation and must be on guard. Shortly after that, I had to have knee replacement surgery.

This also was quite common, and after a few days in the hospital and a few weeks in rehabilitation, I was up and running again. Regrettably, this led to hip replacement surgery some seven months later. The initial hip operation was not deemed a success because of something dopey that I did. As such, the operation had to be repeated three months later.

The orthopaedic surgeon whom I was referred to was highly recommended, and he indicated to me that when he went to do the second operation, all looked normal. In fact, he had difficulty separating the hip joint to replace it. I had confidence in him and started looking at other causative factors.

On release from the hospital, I was haemorrhaging internally. This caused me to be hospitalised immediately for ten days, during which time they were unable to identify what was causing the haemorrhaging. During that stay in the hospital after the second operation, I was diagnosed with blocked arteries that required surgery.

I again looked at the effects of exposure to radio wave sickness or EMF: listed as joint pains, cancer, a burning sensation in the ears and face, itchy skin, and heart attack. Furthermore, the metal used for artificial joints was an excellent conductor that would magnify the effects of electromagnetic radiation. I now had a conductor in my knee and in my hip, one on each side of the body.

Based on that, I slowly began to believe that because the cut tyre did not work, and because I had gone to the authorities, they were using alternative methodologies to shut me up and stop me.

Cancer is increasingly prevalent today and is often a cause of death. A heart attack is another common cause of death, particularly at my age. Nothing suspicious there. If either of these elements could be used to achieve the desired effect, to achieve what would be deemed as a natural and normal process, then they would have achieved their objective without arousing any suspicion.

I had often observed many of the symptoms: itchy skin, falling asleep in front of the TV, and a myriad of other conditions that caused me to believe that I was being targeted for what they thought I knew and could prove in relation to their operations. Now I was strongly convinced they were using EMF as the tool to achieve their objective.

Initially, I had doubts and thought that I was getting carried away with waves of paranoia, imagination, and a series of other thoughts. But time after time, I had to sit down, and after many hours of reflection and collecting my thoughts, I had no alternative but to conclude that I was being targeted and that this was a reality and now their chosen methodology.

I was totally unaware as to how much of a health hazard radiation exposure was. Yet we are exposed to it at work throughout the day, at home at night whilst we are sleeping, and whilst we are outside and close to high voltage power lines. After these incidents, I was becoming increasingly aware and accepting that I needed to learn more.

I identified cell phones. Today, there is one with just about everybody, and increasingly with young children. This is a primary cause for concern because of the intensity of the waves from a cell's internal antenna and its proximity to the head.

This, combined with our total exposure to today's modern tools of computers, add up to an intensity of daily doses of radiation.

During my fact finding, I also discovered that electromagnetic waves overheat living cells and damage DNA, decreasing their capacity to repair. They are the cause of headaches and sleep disorders, lowering memory, learning, and attention capacity. Well, wasn't that a coincidence? These were just some of the factors that caused me to start looking for answers to what I was experiencing.

Added to this, EMF is recorded as lowering the reproduction capacity in both men and women, and it may cause ADHD and autism. Isn't the prevalence of autism increasing today? Further, these electronic fields inhibit the production of melatonin, which can lead to Alzheimer's disease or breast cancer—another area where there appears to be an increase in women.

Is EMF radiation the causative factor of increased side effects in modern living? Does anyone really know? Scientists are increasingly vocal about the harmful effects.

EM waves are especially hazardous to children. Their bone density and immune system are still developing, and they are more prone to absorbing higher levels of radiation.

On reflection, I could identify the effect that radiation was having and the role it had played in my life. I was not sufficiently knowledgeable within this field to fully understand the complete picture. When I talked to friends, my doctor, and other people in relation to this, I soon appreciated that as little as my knowledge was, it was far above the average person. Making progress was a slow, long, arduous process.

I had discovered, as with all things, that people form opinions. They come out of the woodwork to explain to you what an absolute clot you are for holding your thoughts and opinion, insisting that you are wrong. They think you should convert to their opinion. Once more I had to set aside the thoughts of the Shouldabaters and Mustabaters and plot my own path because in my opinion, with the circumstances surrounding me now, I did not feel I needed any further uncertainty around me.

My local doctor was totally unable to help me. Talking to whom I considered to be authorities, such as the CSIRO, was also a pointless exercise. In fact, all I achieved was conflict in what was believed and what was the cause of specific situations. It was from this maze that I finally decided to explore the web, and I identified information about the symptoms I was experiencing.

CHAPTER 35

After all the distractions and false trails that I had traversed, I finally had to accept that I was correct in my initial belief. I had stumbled into something that involved Theo and a variety of others. There were some extremely lucrative and financial benefits being gained by what I could only explain as an extremely simple but effective operation.

One example of this being is farmers and landholders who have worked for generations on their properties, but because of drought and other aspects (common in Australia), they are experiencing hard times. These people, exposed to the system, have lost their properties that have been with them for generations—and quite by coincidence to overseas buyers. Chinese, American, and British were positioned financially to buy these properties.

I was being forced into a position to do the same thing. There is nothing within the regulations that prohibit them from doing so. The requirement for properties or that of farmers or other people in this environment is prone to exploitation using this methodology or system.

Another strange coincidence: the European friend had Chinese buyers to whom he needed property to sell.

Today, as always, young couples scrimp and save to get the deposit to buy their own homes. Once in the home, they're battling to maintain the payments and manage their expenses with young children, a car, and other expenses. Many are living on the edge. If I was positioned to push them over into a default position, and I was positioned to acquire their assets, could I make money out of it? Who could put this into operation?

These are also ideal victims because if they are then put into severe financial hardship, they qualify as candidates to be put through the system.

There are thousands of young people who lose their dreams in this situation. From my investigations, this is a contrived situation where they can do nothing because they are unaware of what is going on around them. Where do you start to prove that something like this is happening? How many people are being affected? Is this what I was told that was worth billions?

CHAPTER 36

I spent many years of frustration and what I thought was delusion and my imagination. Thanks to my European friend, who helped me to finally reach my conclusions, I determined that Theo and his operation was a victim of their own FUD. They were unsure or thought I knew more about their operations than I did. They had doubts as to what I knew about their operations and what I would and could do to jeopardise them. This was common with the position I was in.

After many long years, I could identify that some solicitors involved within the divorce sector were just one part of the operation. More important was the role they played and their importance as to the operational continuation.

Whilst making money themselves, and in many cases large sums, they identified prospective people who could become part of the system by notifying the banks, the heart of the system. This was normal practice in a divorce situation and seen as acting in their customers' best interests.

The solicitors control the divorce process. We are reliant on them to look after our best interests and correctly position us to address our interests. In this situation, they enjoy our trust and our faith. If you and your ex-wife possess any assets, it is at this juncture that you are identified as a potential candidate. If you have a mortgage on your property, as most of us do, the bank is notified of the situation. This notification will filter through the loan department of the bank. At this stage, the required controls will be activated by the loan department. Working in conjunction with the solicitors is guided by the solicitors at critical times.

It was from this initial realisation that I linked the solicitors to the loan department in the bank. From this identification that some bank staff were initiating normal recovery procedures, part of the initiation of recovery was to obtain a valuation of any property. Valuers aware of bank recovery procedures were available to place a valuation on the property. This valuation was slanted directly in the bank's favour because the valuation was often below true market value.

Again, it took me a long time to determine that what I assumed was in the bank's favour might well be in the favour of a bank employee and his connections. The penny only really dropped when my records were interfered with.

Were the banks acting under instructions from above—the controllers? The tier I identified above and controlling the banks. These mystical, mythical people were immersed in the clouds.

The banks or their connections direct the sales process in a manner that enables a buyer to purchase the property below market value. Would it be wrong to assume that the buyer is known to the person involved in the bank's recovery division within the loan department of the bank?

Finally, after many years of wasted time, thoughts, and deductions, I had established the connection between the solicitors and in turn connected the banks to Theo's operation. I identified that this was just one part of the operation. I further identified that potential victims are also identified by the information about them sent by the various feeders, and they are categorised over several factors.

Up to this point, the feeders have completed their respective functions, and it is now handed over to the relevant members within their respective areas.

The structure to control this appears to be normal good business practice. Monitoring and controlling accounts is common sense, quite normal, and essential. But what are the parameters, and what parameters are used to decide just who the players are going to be targeted?

Clearly the risk and vulnerability factors come into play. Statistically, these factors can be identified and monitored. When aware of this, how staff can use this information to their own designated advantage? If payments are delayed by the staff within the lending authority, outside parties can be used and coerced to slow down the situation. Situations are established until the victims' capital is exhausted.

Costs are increased, and a wonderfully designed mechanism comes into play. It's an area I was made painfully aware of during my building project.

All this combined to start putting together a picture that was proving to be correct. Then this basic model, simple but brilliant in concept, could be imposed on a variety of areas in everyday life to incorporate many aspects of our lives and business.

Finally, I had something positive, but I still did not fully understand the sheer size and enormity of what I had stumbled into. The size of the operation frightened me as to what my exposure was. More important, how many of my friends and family were I implicating without even realising what I was doing?

More and more dropped into place. I also realised there was no limiting factor as to the number of people using it. People involved within the financial sector were part of the system and the methodology used to bring about their desired result. Therefore, the cling-ons were using the system to their own advantage. And where did they fit into the operation, both in Australia and internationally?

The System" The Supply Chain—International

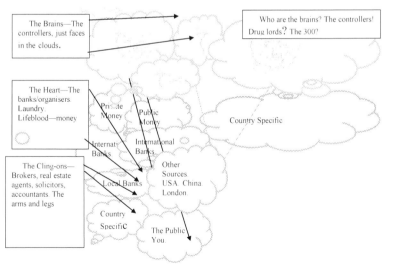

CHAPTER 37

I had now confirmed Theo and his bunch of cling-ons as the number one suspect causing me grief. Furthermore, I had seen and witnessed the immensity of the situation and identified what Theo was doing.

For a person in business who required a loan for business, or as in my case a building project, the logical place he would go to would be a bank, a broker, or an accountant—as I termed them, feeders. They in turn would direct you to the source, the relative department in the bank or the respective money lender. Based on this theory, I nominated the feeders as accountants, solicitors, mortgage brokers, bank branches, real estate agents, and cling-ons.

Cling-ons were many people within the banking and associated industries that were aware of the system's methodology. Each of them had told me to be careful because it went right through to the top.

Cling-ons become or have been made aware of the system and have started their own little business using the basic methodology to their own advantage. They act as feeders. From this, it is apparent that the whole situation is quite widespread. Once they're aware of the working mechanism, they could use it quite freely.

Accepting I was partly right, delusional, extremely imaginative, and all things in between, I started further exploring as to how some of the interference that I was being subjected to could come about. Could my phone conversations and home be invaded electronically? Could I be listened to? And with the wonderful world of electronics, what could be achieved? To this I put a definite yes, but again I went back to the Internet and discovered how this could be directed at me.

I had a mobile phone, landlines, television sets, and computers in operation at home. So what? Most people did. These were controlled and operated by radio waves and Wi-Fi. Today, it's almost impossible to live without it. These devices, including Google, the cloud, and others, become the very tools to enable someone to tap into and investigate your home. They can view, listen, and record your daily activities twenty-four seven. They also provide the tools to examine and record you're every move. Thoughts of privacy, confidentiality, and respect for an individual's rights are now finished.

Recent newspaper reports supported what I had discovered. One of the headlines in the business daily was, "Mortgage Stress House of Horrors." Another article in the *Sydney Morning Herald* on 23 January 2016, was headlined "Property Boom a Drug Cash Target" and written by Heath Aston.

When I saw the size of some of the transactions that were involved in these articles, I thought about how small I was—a small player in this environment in relation to the total scheme of things. I was comforted in some way, knowing that other people were aware of the situation. This confirmed what I had been told by people whom I had spoken to within the banking and financial sector for many months.

This article in the *Sydney Morning Herald* quoted this as being used as a laundry, adding that the property boom was a drug cash target. It reaffirmed what I had become involved in, and after years of speculation and supposition, others were identifying things that supported my beliefs.

In both instances, I was a victim of the system being operated by the cabal. Initially when I was totally unaware of the mechanism, I directed my anger at the solicitors and the methodology. To say I was encouraged to leave my home, go interstate, and not see my daughters for eight years was just one other area I never forgot.

I considered myself fortunate in many ways that I had managed to contact and re-establish a relationship with my youngest daughter. I still remember the day when I stopped seeing them, stopped being a father, and stopped enjoying what a father was meant to enjoy. Children are meant to have love from a father.

Conversely, I could but think on the long-term future effect on my two daughters. On reflection, this was but one side effect of the system designed by those involved within the legal profession. Or was it the legal profession? Were they simply the middlemen in the system?

It did alert me to many aspects of how the system could be used to exploit the unwary. I would be forever grateful to the European gentleman who was attempting to put me through the same process again, but in essence, I classified him as a cling-on who used the system to his own advantage.

Actions such as this, together with the behavioural characteristics he displayed, further confirmed within me that he was involved and aware of the system's mechanism and was using it to his own advantage.

I could not understand the continued harassment that I had experienced for quite some time. This seemed to stop to a degree after a conversation with him when he said, "Mark. what proof do you have about what you said is going on? Proof that I can show somebody else?"

"Absolutely none," I said.

"'So how did you draw these conclusions, and how do you know if you are correct?"

"One, the meeting with Theo started me off. From this I had myself investigated. They identified Theo. Theo confirmed that I was doing something that he wanted me to stop. The threat was very definite. Two, the harassment continued. I continued my investigations by talking to people going through a divorce, friends in banks, and a variety of people in associated industries. I outlined my theories, and they confirmed my beliefs—at the same time telling me to be careful."

"But you have no actual proof?" he said.

"No," I said. "I really cannot prove anything. I never could. In fact, I did not know what this was all about from the start. I went on TV for a totally different matter."

That was the last conversation I had with him.

CHAPTER 38

A mortgage broker is paid a percentage of the value of the loan over the period of the loan. Assuming a loan for one million dollars, he is paid 0.5–0.7 per cent of the loan value for the period of the loan. He is also paid a lump sum initially, again from 0.5–0.7 per cent. This generated an ongoing income stream for the mortgage broker. But this was only part of the system.

If you consider that this loan is primarily provided by the banks and is therefore controlled by the loan department within the banks, this establishes their pivotal role in operating the systems. Being in this situation they can control each loan and monitor the status, vulnerability, and ability of the mortgagee or loan recipient.

Good control in this area is as essential in normal banking as it would be with any debtor's ledger. People establish a trading profile, a credit history. Some border on delinquency at certain times within their loan lifespan.

Another article, Paul Gilder's "Mortgage Stress House of Horrors" in *The Daily Telegraph* highlights that Moody's warns more struggling families to default. Young couples always want to buy their own property, and with the added burden of a young family, cars, and modern living, they have incredible difficulty getting into owning their own home. They are often sailing very close to the limits to maintain their homes.

The article quotes a recent monthly review whereby home loans in arrears climbed from 1.2 to 1.4 per cent between October 2015 and November 2015. This happened in the space of thirty days. The mortgage delinquency rate is predicted to increase, as is the growth in the price of housing.

Whilst Moody's predicted that Australians have been diligent with their mortgage repayments, maintaining a healthy level of household savings since the 2008 financial crisis, things will get tougher in the ensuing years. This is another sector, and opportunities are available for the system to be operated. Young couples do experience difficulties, as we all have over the years, in buying a house, maintaining a car, bringing up a family, and keeping pace with modern living.

Now, suppose that someone in the loans department of the bank was positioned to appreciate the situation and develop ways of further increasing the financial strains associated with a young couple. Suppose that individuals within the loan department are positioned to cause the young couple to default. The bank, being the mortgagor, would have to take reasonable steps to recover the loan (or the assets acting as security for the loan). Repossession is but one of the steps to recover their loan.

Assume that that staff within the loan department already have customer contacts, friends, and associates arranged for just this situation, positioned to buy these properties at a reduced rate. This is what I established as part of the system. A simple action like increasing the percentage rate on a loan by 0.5 per cent would cause delinquency in many cases. Could this be one of the tools used to achieve an objective? So here we have it both ways by the banks. Private money used to finance the loan deposited with the banks. Assume the source is unknown. It's gaining interest, financing a legitimate loan to a customer. The customer is intentionally put into a situation by the finance sector whereby he defaults. The banks must recover the money and exposure; repossession of the bank's assets are initiated. Either the banks repossess, or they sell to a tame buyer below actual market value. Some staff are aware of this operation. Why, then, have they not done something about it? Was it the fear factor? Were they or had they been exposed to the threats that I was? How many were part of it and making money from it? How many were under duress?

I was caught up in something I did not want to be caught in. Furthermore, the harassment continued in simple, subtle ways that affected my everyday lifestyle. It was this combination of actions that brought home to me that I had no alternative but to fight back.

If this meant being found in the back of the car, then so be it. I considered the cost to me, the harassment, and the loss of my two daughters. The other fathers and parents being put through the processes added to my making the decision I did. This was simply my situation. There were thousands caught within, victims of this system, unaware that they were being used as a source of money laundering and, for want of another term, revenue generation. But is it illegal?

I have identified some of the players that were working the system, and there was a cost to them that they had to incur for interfering in my life to this degree. Furthermore, they had done this to me and my family. I had spoken to many others who had gone through what I had. They too had children and families affected by the system. I knew some of the effects that the divorce had on the children. We as parents must share responsibility for the unknown, far-reaching effects that do not surface until many years later, whether financial, physical, psychological, or emotional.

I had established quite clearly how some members of society were exploiting this situation for their financial gain. I knew what Theo did not want me to interfere with.

CHAPTER 39

One of the articles in the *Herald Sun*, by Karina Barrymore, was entitled "ASIC Must Go for Broke-rs". It further confirmed my ever-growing beliefs. Within the article, it stated quite strongly that based on the information provided, the mortgage brokers appear to be on the same self-destructive path as financial planners. It asked whether mortgage brokers are reliable, because they appear to be in sweetheart deals and murky, backhand commissions with the major banks. They obscure payment arrangements and have bonuses, high commissions, holidays, non-cash deals, conflicts of interest, and priority approvals. As a result, the outcome for customers was not as good. The bank culture was infiltrating through to other financial sectors.

The indication was that if you're a small lender or an independent lender, you stand little chance of getting your mortgage recommended through a broker. This is because the banks have stitched up the home loan market with their modus operandi of preferential commission payments and bonuses for selling their products.

As we all know, there is no more important investment for a young couple than buying their house. As such, the article suggests that ASIC is finally looking at the shady side of mortgage broking. The article stresses that the investment watchdog is having a better look at what's going on and how it's going.

It went on to indicate that most banks and institutions pay brokers an upfront commission and an annual trailing commission that lasts for the life of the loan. This is usually a percentage of the loan size; the bigger and longer the loan, the more money the broker makes.

Perhaps belatedly, I recall when I spoke to ASIC in relation to what I thought was going on couple years ago. I felt that this and other reports may or may not be a by-product of what I tried to explain to ASIC.

The Reserve Bank and associated Australian regulators have warned that the quality of many mortgages is now a major issue for the financial system, indicating that home loans are deliberately extended to the maximum number of years, as a result putting the wider economy at risk. Further, loans organised through mortgage brokers incur a much higher default rate than other types of loans.

The article also indicated that behind the brokers, the banks are pulling the strings for what is close to four hundred billion dollars. Brokers accounted for approximately 50 per cent of that figure. As such, commission on that figure approached one billion dollars. Add to this over three hundred million paid each year in trailing commissions until the loans are paid off.

The figures quoted to me initially started to make sense. Until recently, I had difficulty understanding where the billions and trillions of dollars that the banking and mortgage people I had spoken to came from.

An article in *The Australian* on 30 May 2016, "Mortgage Brokers Blame the Banks for Default Rates" by Michael Roddean, indicated that the mortgage market alone is estimated at being worth $1.3 trillion. This started putting some sound perspective into what I had been told. It gave me a little more understanding as to the size of the potential situation. This is my interpretation based on the article.

The article indicates that mortgage brokers blame the banks' underwriting standards for the higher default rates on loans that originate through brokers, and they are hitting back on the key rationale for the corporate watchdog's review of the mortgaging industry and review of the remuneration structure in the broking industry by ASIC.

Two of the larger Australian brokers, Mortgage Choice and Australian Finance Corp, blamed the banks' underwriting standards for high rates of default in arrears in the loans, adding that remuneration paid the broker was a red herring or instability in the $1.3 trillion mortgage market.

A Mortgage Choice executive went on to say that this was more in the underwriting standards of the banks than anything with the remuneration. He further stated, "Brokers don't have the ability to make underwriting decisions; the underwriting decisions are made by the lender, the banks." Mortgage Choice writes more than 50 per cent of the loans for the big four banks, with a lone book of more than $50 billion.

An Australian Finance group executive indicated that this company has a $110 billion loan book and is performing as well as any lender portfolio. He further indicated, "Every loan that a mortgage broker writes follows the strict process." Their securitisation book is performing better than any bank program. He added that his company had over 2,600 mortgage brokers across Australia and that there was no links between commissions paid to brokers and where mortgage flows went. In some cases, the inverse situation existed. (https://myaccount.news.com.au/sites/theaustralian/subscribe.html?sourceCode=TAWEB_WRE170_a&mode=premium&dest=https://www.theaustralian.com.au/business/financial-services/mortgage-brokers-blame-the-banks-for-default-rates/news-story/d15d65116831c274eda86d569129fe88&memtype=anonymous).

All of this supported what I had established and confirmed the involvement of bank staff. Based on what I experienced with the financial sector, the big banks, and the methodologies used to generate revenue, I thought it extremely amusing to see an e-mail from one of the senior officers in one bank stating that he felt his company was dealing with two very unsavoury characters who had no moral compass, and he regarded both parties to the arrangement as devious. He further went on to make a racially prejudicial statement.

When you read the full article of what transpired, it appears that the two people involved in the lawsuit against the bank, which was a substantial amount of over a billion dollars, were being treated to the system.

The article within the *Australian* by Ben Butler, entitled "$1.5 Billion Lawsuit Puts ANZ Bigotry on Trial", highlights a scandal in relation to the ANZ culture that rocked the bank. It is under scrutiny of an alleged sex, drugs, and strip clubs trading room culture that includes laughing at interest rate rigging. It is now embroiled in a row over sexism that saw a leading broker sacked in one of the biggest lawsuits against the ANZ. The people making the claim indicate that the bank sold their 65 per cent stake in a property for less than it was worth in 2011 after seizing it over personal debts.

Does this support what I have been outlining earlier? The bank obviously denied the allegations, and from this comes some very derogatory comments against both the husband and wife in this case, and their race generally.

Cases of this sort confirmed what I have been investigating, and in this case, a bad picture has been painted for the ANZ bank and the four major banks generally.

What, if any, untoward activity cans you accuse the banks of? I had gleaned from many sources that people, properly equipped, can look inside your home and monitor you via your own personal body electrical system, your TV, your mobile phone, and other electrical items. This enables them to listen and record what was being said and view what you are doing twenty-four seven. This was confirmed by Snowden, who is now in exile in Russia.

The good news and the bad news were explained to me very clearly by the South Australian police force when they indicated to me that if anything happened to me, they knew where to go looking, but at this stage there was insufficient evidence for them to open a full police investigation. These comments and similar ones made by Crime Stoppers and the federal police caused ASIC to start their investigation.

At the back of my mind, was a constant feeling that I was becoming more and more embroiled in something where I was way out of my depth. I really didn't want to continue, but I had to stop the constant harassment and interference in my life. I simply wanted to be left to get on with my life.

When I considered my own experiences, together with the information provided within a variety of articles in newspapers, I could relate to the various articles. With the people I had spoken to more closely, I could see a definite link between the real estate market, the divorce market, and the banks involved in divorce and real estate. Then I saw an article in one of the morning papers, entitled "Property Boom a Drug Cash Target", that further reinforced what I had been thinking, dispelling thoughts of imagination and paranoia.

An article by Heath Aston in the *Sydney Morning Herald* described the rampant real estate market as presenting a golden opportunity for criminals to launder millions of dollars in drug money in Australia, based on the information provided by police. There is evidence of criminal cash entering an already inflated housing market to enable properties being bought with proceeds of crime. A report by the New South Wales crime commission claimed that criminal gangs have exploited the property market as surging prices increased demand for funds into Australia. This has provided greater opportunities for organised crime syndicates to launder millions of dollars, the commission found. It enabled the flow of money out of Australia to settle drug transactions using so-called remittance agents to facilitate the movements of entangled legitimate offshore investors in money-laundering schemes.

The article stated there is a very low risk opportunity for organised crime to launder drug proceeds in Australia. Australia must consider stricter rules to control the amount of money pouring into Australia.

Within this article, I identified that federal authorities were considering extending anti-money-laundering requirements that already cover banking remittances and gaming to real estate agents, lawyers, accountants, and precious stone dealers. A combination of articles and reports in the press, together with the discussions I had with my contacts and friends in the banking and finance sector, attributed to me believing that I was but one victim who'd stumbled into the beautifully designed operation that was making billions of dollars from an unsuspecting public. It also emphasised that I was not only talking about Australia but internationally.

It took me many years to realise just what the situation was. The depth and size of what I appeared to be interfering with was further made apparent to me by an article in the *Daily Telegraph* on 2 February 2016 entitled "The Oz Fathers: Down Underworld in Grip of Mafia" by a journalist named Charles Miranda. (https://www.pressreader.com/australia/the-daily-telegraph-sydney/20160202/281479275445364).

Within this article, Italian police have warned that the mafia grip on organised crime in Australia is unbreakable. They indicated that the world's most powerful mafia organisation, Ndrangheta, has Australia divided into six zones, entrenching the drugs and extortion business. Further, Italian police have indicated that organised crime syndicates have infiltrated Australian police forces, including prominent politicians. They do not expect to make a dent in the surface. It stated Australia as one of the countries where these crimes are being consolidated. Further, there are six locales for drug importation as well as large-scale construction contracts, payments of backhanders, and racketeering. It highlights that when building a motorway, you get 1 per cent of a bid and make $10 million without pushing a gram.

All I could think of at this stage was, *Bloody hell. What have I stumbled into. and what have I exposed my family and friends to? Is Macquarie Bank part of this?*

CHAPTER 40

had finally come to realise and recognise that I was but one victim in the system. I saw it being cleverly organised by someone other than the banks or solicitors—but by whom?

The result could really all be pointed at victims, based on their stupidity, lack of ability, inexperience, or a variety of other aspects. But the sophistication of the system, and the people on which the system has been perpetrated by the operators, involved operators who could be regarded as the pillars of our community—staff or people on whose word we rely on for advice and guidance.

As I had discovered, I had been given excellent advice by people within these very areas. From this I did not for one minute believe that all solicitors were enrolled in the system, but if you talk to people going through divorce, you will find that it is still common practice for an adversarial situation to be established. Today, it is much more refined.

I had also established a high degree of similarity in the way that the system was being operated when I was involved in my building project.

Just three doors away from me, Alec started on a very similar building project. He lost the lot. During the many conversations we had, he indicated to me that the builder he had employed was not fulfilling his building commitments and kept asking for additional progress payments. He was then using his progress payments on other projects that he himself was building, not on Alec's building.

Another case I was advised about involved a builder building six hundred units. He too lost the lot. This was not an isolated case.

It became increasingly obvious to me that they were being subjected to the same system that people were trying to put me through. As I investigated further, I found what appeared to be a system being operated by another building group, with money being processed by Middle Eastern companies.

Because of activities that occurred in a nearby locality that can only be regarded as suspect, I decided to stay out of the situation, discretion being the better part of valour.

These incidences and the newspaper articles supported what I believed was in operation, but as I have said, these were things that have happened to me. The disappearance of material from computer was directed at me. I could not in any way take any of this information and show it to a third party. What I identified was happening to others, I could not prove because it was made to look like normal delinquent business transactions. Proving that they were a construed situation was almost impossible.

To illustrate this further, what would be the resultant effect of banks increasing the interest percentage rate? How many loans would become delinquent and cause banks to foreclose to protect their loans? Look at the total marketplace. Home loans are just one potential area. Take that same methodology across small business; they have homes that they are paying off. With farmers and their properties that have been in their families for generations, would Chinese, American, English, or European buyers be interested in these properties? How do you position the property to be placed on the market? Could the controllers or the cling-ons arrange this?

I identified many common denominators. One, the solicitors and those within the legal profession, together with the methodology employed to achieve their objectives. This combination of events caused me to identify the loans department within the bank or banks as having a pivotal role in the operation. It also was one of the primary causes for me to determine these people as the primary suspect for the cause of the harassment that had been maintained on me. I appreciated that whilst people within the banks could become the pivotal factor; they had established many feeders. I had identified the loans department as a central pivot and was advised that knowledge and control of the operation went to the top.

With knowledge of the system, cling-ons and feeders can use many elements of the system to their own advantage. One of these was relatives within a family circle. One instance I identified fell within this sphere. It could have been his occupational aspirations; but he was in a situation whereby he had to travel around the state frequently and stayed overnight in a variety of different places. His whole manner and operating philosophy aroused suspicion within me.

On more than one occasion at family gatherings, I partially overheard conversations between two of the members that aroused my suspicions. My belief was that one person, who worked in the finance company, was but a tool in the hands of the other relative. This was supported by the behavioural characteristics of the person working for the finance company. At family gatherings, he would walk into where I was sitting, make some strange and unusual comments, and then turn around and walk out. It was almost like he had been primed to come in and say what he said.

CHAPTER 41

Whilst I was contemplating the various aspects, I cast my mind back to Stephan, whom I had put down as suspect number two. I had identified that the superannuation money that my father had not claimed (based on the persuasion of this relative) amounted to over one million dollars; this was in the early eighties.

At that time, my father, though comfortable, could not be classed as a rich man. But Stephan and his wife had persuaded my father to not pursue his entitlement of one million dollars on the pretext that it might affect his pension.

I could never understand this line of logic, but it became apparent after my father's death, when Stephan claimed the money for himself.

Again, he was now operating as a financial consultant or mortgage broker, and he'd built a business within that area. His son, who had dropped out of medical school, was also a mortgage broker, and he worked for and took over the business from his father.

I had seen very little of the money from my father's estate, which was controlled by my relatives. The relationship between him and me had long since broken down, and trust was not a factor I had considered. Furthermore, the relationship, having broken down, meant that to a degree, I was somewhat excommunicated from my family.

Through work commitments, I moved and lived interstate from my family and relatives. I did not experience a family life as a young man. My parents had separated, and I lived with my father until my early teens, in lodgings. When I was transferred interstate; not seeing much of my family was nothing new because I had experienced this most of my life.

I had established, through the series of situations that I had lived through, that my harassment could have been caused from one of these parties. Independent on the situational factors surrounding me, I had numbered them suspect one as most likely, suspect two as less likely to be connected, suspect three as less likely connected, and suspect four as least likely.

As serious as the situation was, I used to sit down and chuckle at some of the times when I went on full alert. The expectation that something was about to happen and the surrounding circumstances would add cause to my belief, only to find that that I was the one who'd made a mistake.

One instance that I remember was when I woke at about seven one morning. Prior to that, a couple of days before, I had to take my car and leave it for another of the inexplicable events or causes for repairs. Because of this, my car was not parked outside as it usually was. This was not that unusual because I was often out prospecting or ego building, and as such I'd stay at a friend's house. But for all intents and purposes, for someone looking outside, my car was not there, and so I was not home.

I was lying in bed and contemplating my success, or lack thereof, on my prospecting efforts the previous evening. It was then that I thought I heard part of a ring on my phone. I also thought I had heard my front door opening shortly after, and this put me on full alert. For the previous twelve months, I was training at hap Ki do three nights a week and Saturday afternoons. I was very fit and ready, tensed up for action. I quietly put on my tracksuit and positioned myself just around the corner from the front door. The phone rang, and I ignored it, I was tense and ready, waiting for whoever came through the front door to walk into my kitchen. I was still waiting as the phone stopped ringing. The phone started ringing again, and so I decided I'd better answer it.

As it turned out, it was a friend wanting to know if I was going to church that morning. After I finished and hung up, I reflected on what they had put me through. Despite what was going on around me, I had let myself get into this frame of mind. The front door was wide open, and so I assumed that I had heard it being opened prior to the phone ringing.

It was then that I decided if I was going to believe in the guy with the shepherd's crook and the long flowing gown, and if I had decided that I wanted to go on living, I should do what I had been told: hand the problem over. Peace of mind returned. This Christian bit was new to me, so I was vacillating a bit.

CHAPTER 42

"They know when you're sleeping. They know when you're awake." These were the words used by Edward Snowden, stating that all of us are under observation twenty-four hours a day. When you go onto the web, whom you talk to, the frequency of calls, all your daily activities, the pattern of life—all of this is recorded. This is part of what they call metadata, or private records. This is held for a very long time under the metadata retention laws. The police can look up these records (*The Sydney Morning Herald*, 26 May 2016, https://www.smh.com.au/opinion/they-know-when-youre-sleeping-they-know-when-youre-awake-20160526-gp4cei.html).

This article, together with the information provided to me, added further confirmation to what I had believed for a long time. The belief that I held was that if people were interested in you for whatever reason, they could gain access to you and your information. Whilst you're in the comfort and security of your home, every detail can be tracked. Based on that, when Theo told me, "We will be watching you," the significance of that remark came home to me very strongly. The strange occurrences and the unusual happenings fell into place.

Never at any stage did I consider the true meaning. I was never equipped to understand to what Theo was referring. I had witnessed, in the early stages, people who obviously were being paid to track my movements—private investigators. I did not at any stage, until comparatively recently, truly believe that I was under close surveillance. The reasons were many and varied: self-doubt, belief that it was my imagination—these were just some of the elements that diverted my thoughts from inescapable fact. This continued until physical facts that I could not deny found by me.

I was introduced to a whole new side of life of which I was totally ignorant. In many ways, I wished I could have been positioned to stay that way.

In Jerusalem, people go and talk to a wall; from this, they achieve their expectation of assistance from their associated belief system. I did not have the time, money, or ability to go to Jerusalem, but I felt talking to the various authorities could provide the same capability. I did this in conjunction with going into my garden and talking to the walls and trees I had built on my property. It more than adequately provided the equivalent of going to Jerusalem at a fraction of the cost.

A frequently asked question from all these authorities was, "What proof do you have?" All too soon, it became apparent to me that I had none. It could all be written off as my vivid imagination, paranoia, and similar mental disorders. Incidences and occurrences happened to me, either in and to my car, my flat, and other venues. But they happened to me. There were no witnesses.

CHAPTER 43

I n just one area, I had established from personal experience a source for potential money. It was within the divorce industry. This is very large supply. The organisations and people had decided that divorcing couples are ideally situated and exposed to be exploited by the system—a subtle, ready market.

As I had explained earlier, the solicitors and those involved within the banking or financial sector are using this as one method of operation in the system. Take this same methodology to people establishing or operating a business, and I could see the exposure of these people to the system.

If you consider the number of people today who have gone into business, when it's is a young business, they have a full-time operation attempting to make that business successful. Their thoughts are consumed by being successful and growing their business, This occupies a large part of their thoughts daily, and it is directed at being a success and surviving. Consider these types as applicable for another potential candidate for the system. They often use their homes and other assets as security.

If the business is exposed to the system, they lose the lot. Are they the biggest bunch of clots for letting his happens to them? They take all the flack. But what do they lose? Their assets and home. They gain a myriad of other psychological disturbances. My investigation suggested that this situation was often contrived.

Now consider the number of people in the general population who have purchased a house, have a young family, and need to maintain one or two cars to support their lifestyle in today's world. Increasingly we hear of mortgage stress and default. Again, from what I have been researching, this is a contrived situation; causing me to say that the banks are but a tool or the heart of the system. They are not the brains.

I have identified just some areas of the general population who are prone to be victims of the system. What are the common denominators? Who is common to all these areas?

It is a safe assumption that they would have a bank loan or finance of some description behind each of them. The probability of an accountant and a solicitor assisting and advising them is very high. This is to be seen to protect them and their financial exposure, and to guard against situations that would force them into default. These and other associated areas form part of the supply chain. Individually, each of these areas would show a comparatively small return if they were to be processed through the system. But look at each area collectively, and look at the total number of people going through a divorce or trying to operate a small business. Think of the number of everyday households in today's economy. The default rate is increasing daily. Are these people prone to being exploited by the system?

It is very easy for us to blame the banks and big business—the rich people exploiting the lesser positioned individuals. But consider that there are large sums of private money being brought into and used in Australia. Who provides the ideal vehicle for all this private money to be used? Would it be safe to assume that the banking or financial sector in Australia, as it does overseas, would provide the ideal vehicle?

If this money is coming into Australia, and it is private money, where is it coming from?

I had already had it explained to me that one of the factors was that the casinos were being used to launder money. Recently, there were several newspaper reports advising of many Italian people involved, generating large amounts of money through drugs.

I had been threatened that I would be found in the back of a burnt-out car or sent back to my wife with my face rearranged. I was aware of similar threats made to other people.

I recalled my thoughts and feelings at the time when Theo initially threatened me: a frightening mix of emotions. But it took me years to identify the connection with what Theo was attempting to hide.

Progressively, I identified and was positioned to connect the various links in the chain as to how the system operated.

Think of a situation where you work and are offered the opportunity to make some extra money on the side.

You have access, and it may be as simple as giving some information that you can access to someone who requested it and is prepared to pay you money for that information.

Say you work at the motor registry, and I am prepared to pay you one hundred dollars for the name and address of the owner of a car. You are positioned to look up registration details daily as part of your job function. As such, you can determine and provide what is required to the person requesting the information. The risks are minimal because it is a part of your normal, everyday job function. From that point on, you are locked in.

Whilst I was learning to become a private investigator, I never ceased to be amazed at what information I could find out by simply talking to a person's neighbours. Furthermore, I was surprised at the number of people who would trade information for a financial return. I also learned to be wary of some people close to you. People who you trust are well positioned to provide information to someone who could find it beneficial—a close friend, a relative, a work associate, your next-door neighbour, someone who comes into your daily existence.

If your wife or husband is going to have an affair, remember that up to 75 per cent of married couples do have an extramarital affair, as was my experience during my single years.

It is normally someone whom you trust as part of your circle or family: your brother-in-law, your friend, a relative, an associate, a friend's partner. These were just some of the people identified when I was learning to be a private investigator.

It was also confirmed in my private life when I used to sit back and observe the games people played. It was always a source of amusement and often an eye-opener to watch the various aspects in operation.

From this, I had come to accept that in many areas such as this, if you have any suspicions, always look inside first before you go outside to look for abnormalities and names of suspects. Based on my experiences and my training, that is where you are going to find what you're looking for.

This combination of events enabled me to see situations of this type in my workplace: opportunities presented to me, opportunities presented to associates, friends in a social gathering. Studying the behavioural characteristics of people became a pleasant, interesting pastime. Several times, it proved that a man's ego was a common weakness that could be used and exploited by someone who had an ulterior motive.

I had noticed that this mode of operation had become somewhat common, and not to take advantage of these opportunities when they arose was classified as naive.

This tag caused me little if any concern. I had seen and experienced many areas of this type of situations and knew that it was not an area that fitted into my perception of being a part of the *you* factor.

CHAPTER 44

n several instances, I have identified that we are subjected to a high degree of subtle manipulation by what is done, what we do, and how we do it.

How many adults today have a distorted view of the realities of life based on what we, as parents, have put them through? The French say, "C'est la vie," which can be interpreted as "That's life," or using the Australian vernacular, "Shit happens."

Many people I had spoken to, both counsellors and advisers, told me that children get over a divorce quickly and handle it incredibly well. This was not my experience based on the number of people that I had spoken to and where I had seen the effect on the children of divorce. I saw little evidence that the children handled the situation well.

I often had the opportunity to look at people who had come from a broken marriage, compared to those who had come from a happy family background.

When one considers the increasing number of divorces, marriages, and relationships that have broken down where the parties have elected to separate, it would be fair to assume that there are several people involved in a separation. The bank, accountants and solicitors, real estate agents, and the associated Shouldabaters and Mustabaters come out of the woodwork at times of family crises to tell you what you should or shouldn't do, based on their wisdom and experience. This is liberally spiced with good intentions based on their perception of what they see is being best for you.

Add to this mix some good, old-fashioned FUD. When FUD is added to the equation, this causes you to switch from the left brain (reasoning and logic) into right brain, triggering emotions and feelings that further confuse an already emotionally confused state of mind. You often doubt yourself and embark on the elements within the FUD factor.

Fear is often a trigger for anger, another element. You have created for yourself a harmful mix of psychological emotions. This is somewhat of a catch-22 situation because whilst you are embroiled in this emotional state, it is extremely difficult to switch into logical reasoning and assume a balanced perspective.

It was during these times of emotional turmoil that I had to remind myself that I, like all of us, was a totally unique individual who had been given gifts as part of my make-up. I possessed individual qualities that no other person on earth possessed. I had been given gifts at birth for a reason. These gifts were given to me to be used and not set aside. It becomes my responsibility to identify these gifts and attributes I have been given, and to use them for the reasons given.

I view this as a law of the universe, or it could be my Christian belief. It was always there when the chips were down, and I have stood up against adversity.

This was reinforced during my building project and when I really identified the length and breadth of the system. This was where I identified that the system was designed to put me into a situation where I would be forced to sell.

Once sold, each respective player would be paid a percentage: people at the banks controlling this aspect, the people they employed to evaluate the real estate property, and the various cling-ons such as the real estate agents and those associated with the system. I had identified that this concept was in operation and was used on young couples experiencing the same difficulties that we all face with everyday life. If they could be put into a situation of delinquency, who would be the beneficiaries? Who was holding the mortgage? Who had the tools to monitor and control the situation? Once more, was this a normal financial transactional situation, or was this a contrived situation?

My initial belief was that this was the banks; they were the rotten scoundrels, in the same league as the divorce solicitors. I had enough people involved with the banks tell me that the bank culture was to disregard what was in the best interests of the customer to promote the delinquent accounts and concentrate on the concept of making money.

I had also established that there were many people within the banking system more aware of the situation, but for any one of a dozen reasons, they would not or could not say anything about it. I had spoken to mortgage brokers and people working within the banks; they had verbally provided me with information. They had advised me and corrected me when I thought in terms of millions of dollars. They were the ones who told me that I should be thinking in terms of billions and trillions of dollars.

At present in society, it is the people's perception that the banks are the scoundrels in this environment. In fairness to the bank staff, consider them being offered a financial incentive to participate and use a methodology, or as with the staff in a motor registry office, to provide information. Also consider that they may have received threats if they didn't cooperate and operate the system as they were required to do. They are but another cog in the machine being operated and designed by a higher authority.

This begs the question: who would have the ability? And what is the incentive? What is the objective of those in a position to exercise this type of control?

Are they the people who designed and implemented the system as another money-making venture being operated in Australia and overseas? By whom? Some say it's the accepted few.

From what I could see, banks were the go-betweens being controlled or manipulated by the controllers.

I had identified the system in operation in three areas: the general population, divorcing couples, and businesses. Added to this were farmers who had difficulty in times of drought. Building developers were using the same methodology of the system, catered around the financial structure and your financial situation—a-controlled situation.

In establishing this conclusion, I looked very closely at the Australian bank ownership tree. From this I also established that there were two primary sources of money coming into Australia: public and private money. Consider this. If you had a large sum of money to invest, clearly you would have to consider the financial institutions and their offshoots as a vehicle. The banks, based on their ability, provide the ideal vehicle to act as a go-between for you, the customer, and the source of finance. In fairness to the banks, they are being used as a vehicle.

From this, it would be unfair to paint all banks as rascals. It would also be unfair to paint all those associated in the financial structure as using the methodology to feather their nests. However, clearly there are those whom I labelled as cling-ons. They know how to use the system to their own advantage.

This appeared to be slightly different to the one illustrated earlier in my research, but it did illustrate and confirm my research and information in relation to the operation of banks, as indicated in an article by Ed Vulliamy, "Global Banks Are the Financial Services Wing of the Drug Cartels". The article supports the theories outlined by my investigations. Contrary to the conclusions invited by the extremely informative paper, the title does sound as if the financial services play a secondary role in the tandem.

Australian Bank Ownership Tree

The tree looks at the overseas ownership of Australia Banks. The companies at the top of the tree are the top four shareholders for all the banks in the following level. The percentage shown is the total ownership the Australian companies have of that bank.

A 2012 report by the Australian Prudential Regulation Australian Authority revealed that the big four—ANZ, Commonwealth, National Australia Bank, and Westpac—are majority owned by the same nominee companies.

These schematics show how the banks are designed to operate in Australia. It also depicts the interest that overseas banks have in Australia and the control that they can exercise on the Australian banking sector.

For the Australian public, home, business, mortgage borrowings, and investment borrowings are sourced by the banks and associated companies in Australia.

Overseas Banks

Private money/public money. Source of money brought into and generated in Australia. Chinese, Italian, Lebanese, Greek, the United States, and ...?

Overseas banks. HSBC, JP Morgan, NAB Citibank.

A 2012 report by the Australian Prudential Regulation Authority revealed that the four banks (ANZ, NAB, Westpac, and Commonwealth) are majority owned by the same nominee company.

Australian Banks: ANZ (49.23%), National Bank (43.09%), Westpac (42.85%), Bank of Queensland (38.21%), Commonwealth Bank (36.75%), Bendigo Bank (28.49%)

Whenever I looked at this diagram, it begged the question: where does the Macquarie Bank fit into this picture? From my reading, the Macquarie started in Australia and has since spread overseas. They have financed major projects such as the construction of motorways, parking stations, major construction, and a variety of large financial requirement projects.

Have they infiltrated the public service sector? Do they have influence over the awarding of state and federal contracts, as depicted earlier?

Herein lay the mechanism used to generate income in the wonderful world of finance. Our criticism has been for the banks. They are making large amounts of money at the expense of the public. Is this strictly true, or are they a vehicle, used by overseas and Australian controllers to increase their return?

How is this done? Who provides the ideal vehicle to generate revenue?

You and your loan payments are monitored and recorded; a history is built of your operational record, credit status, and credit history.

If you fall within the predetermined parameters established by the bank, and if you fit the pattern determined by the bank loans and bank management, you may be a potential victim of the system. If you fall within this category, your payment pattern is identified, and your ability is processed to become part of the system, you are invited into the system! Many situations are escalated beyond your ability to pay. Therefore, the respective parties suggest in the case of a divorce that you may wish to finalise the divorce status, sell your property, and make all necessary arrangements with your ex-wife. Seeking an end to the turmoil in your life, peace returning is a pleasant outcome.

The primary objective of the system is to acquire your assets at below market price. Once you're out of the way, your assets may be sold again at a true market value. Therein lies the profit percentage on this type of transaction.

Take this same system methodology and impose it on young couples struggling to make ends meet or running and operating a business. Add older couples who are not getting enough money to live on, based on interest rate cuts and fluctuations. Are they not prone to being operated on within the system?

Wouldn't this all appear as bad financial management by the respective parties? Consider a developer who is building a block of units or many blocks of units. As mentioned previously, he had six hundred units and was put through the system. Imagine the loan value for building six hundred units, as well as the land and asset value of the units once they were sold or repossessed. Can this be a contrived situation?

Now consider that I am your bank. I set my computer system to identify and report on loans that could default if they had an interest rate rise when they fell within the parameters I had established. Suppose this happened to you. What effect will this have on your financial situation?

I need to set the stage before I do this. How would I achieve this? From a banking perspective, it is so simple. I put up the interest, and people default. I hold the loan, so I repossess. I might have a contact and can arrange to buy your property below the value of what you owe me. As the bank, I can control the situation. I can sell your property to recover the money I lent you. You might still owe me money, and so now I initiate recovery procedures. You have lost your assets and owe money to me. I am pursuing you to recover my money. You might have other debts that you cannot pay, and they are pursuing you too.

Oh, you have a young family that you are trying to bring up. What would be your state of mind, or your relationship with your wife? How would you feel?

These methodologies are in operation overseas, and they operate in the areas that I have identified. What is the combined revenue potential? It exceeded my capacity to fully understand. What had I got myself into?

The process of putting me through the system was simplified because there were a variety of costs that I never anticipated; these were changed and increased during the cost of my building. This is standard fare. Costs are created for you. Comparatively speaking, I was small fry—fruit for the cling-ons or lower echelon.

We are constantly being told of foreign money coming into Australia to acquire real estate. This also applies to New Zealand, Canada, the UK, and parts of Europe. Recognise the laws of supply and demand. The supply of houses to meet the demand generated by overseas buyers cannot keep up.

This is assisting the growth of the property bubble. If you can use the system to satisfy this demand created by overseas buyers and put people into a situation who are forced to sell their properties, you have one way of satisfying demand. Accept that this is a contrived situation. Are young couples a target? Is there an increase in defaults today?

If a borrower wants to borrow money from the banks, take it as several million dollars. The mechanism exists for the developers to be given the money and then have the property repossessed. Is the developer making a percentage of this as payment for the development and increasing the value of the asset, but then returning the asset to the original lender? Could this not be another method of the system in operation once more?

If this happens once in a multi-storey development or a multi-unit development, they are talking several million dollars. If this happens several times, how many millions of dollars are involved?

Suppose I have made a few million dollars through drugs. This money is deposited with the banks. Depositing and investing money are part of the business of the banking industry and their everyday business.

I deposit this money in a bank. Then if my money is used in this manner to acquire assets, the return on my investments would increase dramatically over time. The police have already indicated that they are almost powerless to stop the importing and sale of drugs in Australia.

When working with overseas police, they can only hope to pick up a small percentage of the total drug market. Again, it's reported on by the press in Australia. It has also been reported that Australia acts as a conduit for drugs from South East Asia, Afghanistan, and other countries.

When I was on TV talking about a change to divorce laws to give the non-custodial parent a better situation with their children, I was advised to stop going on television and to not continue with this approach for Children of Divorce.

More recently, I was further advised that he would be sent back to my wife with my face rearranged.

This appeared to be a common and consistent operational methodology. So take this methodology, or alternatively a financial incentive given to operatives within the banking sector, and you have a persuasive tool to help staff within the banking sector comply with your request.

I had also been approached by one of the staff where I was previously employed—let's call him Bill. He said if I really wanted to make some money, I would be assisted by him. However, I would need to pay him 10 per cent of my earnings. Furthermore, recently I was invited to join the movement that was being launched against some orthopaedic surgeons and work with the group to seek financial compensation for what appeared to be neglect on their part. This appeared to me as another money-earning venture directed against successful practices.

Based on what had happened to me, I felt it would be easy if this type of methodology was to be used on bank staff to persuade them to do what was requested of them. In addition to this, I was also offered a situation whereby I would be paid an incentive to join their group to sue the orthopaedic surgeon.

The first incident when I was threatened—that I would be found in the back of the car—happened many years ago. The threat that I would be sent back to my wife with his face rearranged was more recent. The people I had talked to in the banking system were aware of what appeared to be going on, and they indicated that it'd started over thirty years ago. This was consistent with when I was initially threatened.

Further investigation of bank ownership led me to an article that depicted the bank ownership tree and indicated that the Reserve Bank of Australia was wholly owned by the Australian government. That is, until you establish that the logo of the Commonwealth Bank of Australia is a private company, registered by the Securities Commission in Washington, DC. The great Seal of Australia is also registered in the United States.

This organisation has shares for holding banks so that the Australian banks form part and parcel of the company in the United States. It has nothing to do with the Australian government.

If this information is as accurate as it appears, how much control do we have in Australia of the banks? How much control do the banks have of Australia?

Based on this, I went back with the concept of who controls whom. It confirms my position that the banks are extremely powerful but are just one cog in the financial structure. If you look at the banking structure, the overseas names in the bank ownership tree appeared to be HSBC, JP Morgan, NAB, and Citigroup.

Based on this, one must wonder if the banks are a private enterprise. Are their business operation any different than other business operations? What controls are within Australia when a large part of their shareholding is owned by a company or companies registered in the United States?

If we accept that this is the banking structure and who controls this business; it is but one short step to see how undesirable elements can infiltrate and control the financial sector or the banking situation. If we add to this mix the Macquarie Bank in Australia and the operations that they control and finance in the building development sector, roads, and transport development, then who controls and profits from their success?

We have seen evidence and reports in the press from heads of government, both state and federal, leaving their relative government positions and becoming consultants with the bank. If we look further, we can identify a linkage between money being given by unions to political parties to further their cause. There are indications that this has been done to senior government bodies in the past, and it is continuing to be done.

When you consider the actions and the operations of the financial sector as displayed and recorded, you must wonder if the financial sector is but a tool to satisfy the requirements of the 1 per cent. Is it the superrich, the 1 per cent, who want to exercise control and dominate the Western world structure? Is Australia part of an internationally well-designed and well-operated washing machine?

I saw the banks as only a part of the overall system, with the flow of money being distributed from the lower echelons of the structure right up to the top. Or look at the banks as the heart of the system, controlled by the brain. This would need to embrace businesses, people within government departments, and associated areas.

All I had to determine now was where the top was and who controlled it. More important, was this all a figment of my imagination? Of this was not so, why were the harassment and threats continuing?

CHAPTER 45

had discovered many years ago that if you want to exert pressure or interfere with someone's life, you establish contact with somebody they trust—a neighbour or close relative.

I had purchased two monitors to detect radio wave emissions, and each time I turned them on, I established that there were emissions coming from my next-door neighbour's house. This could have been quite innocent because waves are in the atmosphere always; these emissions are transmitted via mobile phones, TVs, and other similar equipment. Add to this the behavioural characteristics of the individual people.

In addition, both of my pieces of equipment that I used to use to detect radio wave emissions had been destroyed by that son of a bitch called "somebody", whom we all have as a resident in our houses. The resultant effect was that I was unable to use these for radio wave detection.

Furthermore, two electrical switches in my house show evidence that someone had tried to prise the cover off and damaged the surrounding paintwork, leaving a small indentation mark.

I did not do this, and so it was more evidence of somebody in my house. One day I was going to catch that son of a bitch

I believed that this neighbour was receiving money to obtain and pass information to somebody else. This reminded me of where to go and whom to talk to when I was doing my training as a private investigator. I certainly did not see any of the behavioural characteristics from this person that indicated he was anything more than a drone or a feeder.

I discovered that with today's electronic capability, someone does not have to come into your house to do what my trainer called "naughty things".

Many years before, I identified a relative whom I did not trust. He came into my life as a member within this family circle and had access to my computer. His actions and personal characteristics caused me to form the opinion that I would be much safer living with a brown snake than I was with this relative.

Information provided to me by an acquaintance who knew both the relative and his ex-wife very well further confirmed my belief that this person did not meet the attributes that I held in high regard. He was more closely aligned to a scheming, sly individual, causing me to suggest to my wife that I did not want this person to enter my house in my absence.

Alec had all the technical capabilities to utilise the tools provided by electronics such as computers, phones, and landlines to spy and invade a person's personal life.

I could have been totally incorrect in placing Alec on the suspect list, but he displayed all the attributes of the people using the system as a cling-on. I believed he had come across the system in operation or had been a victim of the system, and he had decided to use the system to his own benefit.

I had witnessed incidents when he was using another relative as a drone. He would come in, make remarks to me, and then leave my presence. It never failed to amuse me to watch the operations that Alec's drone displayed, or the method in which he behaved. This caused me to believe he was operating under a series of instructions. I partially overheard a couple of conversations between the feeder and Alec on two occasions; one was at a dinner party we attended. I was inside listening to their conversation below the window I was standing in front of.

This incidence did an excellent job of alerting me to the sincerity of Alec within my family circle. Further investigations revealed more each day, causing me to ask myself, whether he was part of the bigger operation and working with the system under their direction. Or was he simply a cling-on?

Whilst investigating these relatives, their behavioural characteristics, and their other attributes, I did not identify any of the attributes required to be part of a large, organised system. More important, I was to be part of the design of an organised system;

I did see that they had all the attributes of a lower strata user or cling-on. This, together with what I had been advised about his operational characteristics prior to coming into my circle, confirmed that he was a con man who had been preying on the weaknesses of single and married women. He certainly displayed a high degree of incongruence in his behaviour, and he possessed all the attributes that I was wary of.

CHAPTER 46

fter many months of studying and analysing the situation that I was in, I was always wary of analysis paralysis, when I looked at the way radio waves could be used to achieve a purpose. I believed that if I compared the various aspects that I had seen and heard, there were elements within our society that used a variety of mechanisms to earn money—in this case, at the expense of an unsuspecting public.

I had the misfortune of being caught up in a couple. From this, I felt that accusing the banks of these anomalies was inaccurate; there was a much broader picture that had to be provided for.

If you look at the banks and liken them to the human body, they are the heart, an essential element or centre of the financial structure. If your heart fails, your whole body shuts down. The brain and all various essential systems, the nervous system, the lymph system, and other systems transmit information and feedback to and from the brain from the various parts of the body. All of this is kept operative by the vital flow of blood through the various aspects of the body.

At times, some part of this could become impaired or break down, and we know of the side effects of this situation. A blocked artery requiring stents, a bypass, a heart attack, cholesterol, and lack of the required exercise—these are just some examples.

However, the essential control is your heart. It pumps blood around your entire system. If the heart stops, everything shuts down.

Imagine the banks as a central control point, or heart, of the financial system. It's a vital essential element within our financial structure. If you removed or impaired the banks, the financial system would stop.

The heart is controlled by the brain's functions, and as we have seen, if part of the brain function is impaired, this may not affect the heart; the heart will keep beating. Working. in conjunction, think of arms, legs, hands, eyes, the nervous system, and all other parts of our body receiving and sending messages back to the brain.

If we use this as an analogy and look at the financial system structure not only in Australia but overseas in America and in Western society, we have seen the influence of outside sources on the financial or banking structure internationally. Are they the heart or the brain? To me, these resources form part of the brain. The critical element is control, and as such they are positioned to exercise a high degree of control over a country's entire financial structure. Then look at that on a global scale. If we control the financial structure of human beings, we have control of society.

We can dictate their actions, control their everyday lives, and control their very being.

I had no concept of how my getting onto TV and talking about non-custodial parents was going to affect their situation. It wasn't until many years later that I appreciated that part of the spoils of the divorce was the acquisition of the assets in the process. I could not even begin to imagine the scope and size of this operation.

I had firmly established use of radio waves or electromagnetic radiation as a tool against me. This was the adopted methodology after the cut tire, and other interferences with my car and threats had not succeeded.

This had all been shown, reported to the police, and recorded as to whom I thought was responsible. The police advised me that if something happened to me, they knew where to go looking.

I realised that to achieve their objectives, they had to shut me up. The added benefit of all aspects was to make it look like normal situational circumstances. The heart attack could all be brought on by increasing the radio waves to cause damage, via the insertion of a conductor within my body.

This was done through knee and hip replacement surgery. As such, in a period of fifteen months, I underwent knee replacement surgery, which triggered hip replacement surgery. The hip replacement surgery had to be done twice because it appeared that it was not done correctly. Within days of leaving the hospital after the second hip replacement surgery, I had to visit my surgeon for a check-up after the operation.

I then suffered restrictions in his chest, which caused the surgeon to have me immediately hospitalised for fear that a blood clot had formed. I was also suffering from heavy internal bleeding. Medical staff were unable to determine the cause.

It was during this period that they identified I was required to have two, and possibly three, stents inserted into the veins going into my heart, with over 90 per cent blockage. This was required somewhat urgently, and I had to restrict my movements until the stents were inserted shortly afterwards.

Once more, it was all normal and natural in appearance; heart attacks happened every day, and people were diagnosed with cancer every day. Was this a shade of paranoia? Or was this the alternative methodology after the other methods had failed?

During all this time, and for several months preceding the series of events, I was studying the effects of radio wave sickness. I found that I would feel nauseous after I switched on my computer. While driving my car relatively short distances, I would have pain in my major joints, hips, knees, arms, and hands. I would fall asleep suddenly in front of television or while sitting down and relaxing. I was constantly woken up at about three o'clock each morning and so would fall asleep at about the same time in the afternoon. I would hear a click, such as light switch that had been turned on from one of the power points. I had also noted at certain times that I would get a partial ring on my phone. The indication was that someone was trying to put a tap on my phone.

Through my research, I had established that a lot of the symptoms that I had were a by-product of radio wave sickness. Feelings of nausea, aching joints, headaches, flushed feeling in the face, itching, interference from TV, the inability to concentrate, memory loss—these were just some of the symptoms that I experienced as a by-product of radio wave exposure.

I discovered that talking to my doctor was a waste of time. As previously mentioned, I might as well talk to the wall. All of this could be attributed to a natural situation. People at my age have blocked arteries, suffer from arthritis, and suffer memory loss and confused thinking. All of this is considered a normal occurrence for people getting older.

I used to doubt myself until one day I woke up. My being threatened was no allusion. That was not a delusion. I was being woken up between two and three each morning. I wasn't imagining feelings of nausea when I drove my car, and neither did I imagine the sound of what appeared to be a tape recorder winding in my car. I didn't imagine a cut mark left on the handle of the handbrake in my car. Neither did I imagine somebody else's body odour when I first went down to my car.

I moved interstate in the belief that if I got out of the situation I had created, then things would settle down.

My appearance on TV to explain the situation of fathers once a fortnight seemed to be the trigger that created these reactions against me. It was only recently that I finally connected the dots in the various areas that were affected. The system was widespread, operating in many areas and under many guises. But it was out there.

CHAPTER 47

I was astounded when I read an article entitled "Escaping the Matrix" by Richard Moore. It was directed at how we can change the world. Within this article, it refers to us waking up from an illusion and suddenly realising that everything was quite different than what we thought. He went on to discuss what he classed as the consensus of reality, which we see portrayed on television and in school history books, as a fabricated delusion. The lies of politicians are repeated in the media and then become the basis of history. He further illustrated that the war in Iraq provides an excellent example because it is depicted as bringing democracy to the Iraqis. The United States are seizing control of petroleum resources to establish a permanent military outpost in the Middle East.

Moore talks about the history of humanity as being different than what we are taught at schools. He characterises a civilisation by hierarchy and centralised governance. Further, he states that our evolution has been driven by a dog-eat-dog competition. This is a contradiction to early civilisations and is not a reflection of human nature. It is rather a system of domination and exploitation by the ruling elites.

Compare this situation, as outlined, to what we see operating in society today. When we see a number of people from many walks of life being taken advantage of as an unsuspecting public, and by people we are forced to put our trust and faith in, we must look at the financial structure today and how we see it in operation.

If a business is to operate as a business and be successful, it must make a profit. This is a must do if banks are to continue to provide us with the finance we need. But if we examine the operations of the cling-ons and the feeders operating within the bank and financial system, we find that these are really elements that can only be described as organised extortion or a situation that encourages deceit and deception.

Reverting to supply and demand, one of the basic economic tenants, there is an acute shortage in the supply of affordable housing and real estate to satisfy the demand created in Australia. This is not just in the real estate sector. Daily we hear about a real estate bubble, and we hear of Australian land, businesses, and assets being sold to overseas buyers. For one moment, consider whether the real estate bubble is a construed situation. If thousands invest in real estate, and then you now have a loan for a property you are renting out, and then the interest rate is increased, your expenditure exceeds your income. You must sell. You are prone to the system.

From a business point of view, this is the opportunity for us to generate revenue in Australia. To maintain the supply, one must recognise the questionable methodologies used to provide the supply of housing, as well as assets to satisfy the demand.

If the feeders, the cling-ons, and the system are to make money from this source of finance, then they need to acquire assets that they can resell to return a profit. This is where the system's methodologies are used on a range of the Australian public, in order to provide the asset base that can be sold to overseas buyers. If we accept that Australia is relatively small fry and regarded as billions or perhaps trillions of dollars in revenue, what is the size of the international market—and who are the organisers?

Having accepted that the banks and financial structure are the heart of the system and that the supplier funds are vast and from many different origins, we can see how and why supply needs to be generated to satisfy the demand.

Richard Moore talks about we the people are the transformational imperative. He talks about a chronic cancer that has plagued us for six thousand years. He then goes on to say that there is no one person who can bring about the radical transformation that is required to save humanity and the world. However, it is a job that must be done, and we must do it for ourselves.

I could do nothing but agree fully with this position, the situation, and what must be done. He questioned the ability of us as a society to bring about change. Based on this statement, how do we address the situation whereby the Australian public are being placed in a financial situation and are forced to divest their assets to survive? It's a situation being orchestrated by the controllers.

During a recent election in Australia, there was the strong cry for a royal commission into the banks. A royal commission into the banks would be an investigation into the operations of the heart—a heart beating to a drum played by the brain.

The heart is not in control by itself, but it does control many aspects. There is a high degree of control exercised by the brain or controllers. The mind and body interact in many ways that affect a person's health—or in this case, wealth. The brain is the central control point of all associated systems, and therefore investigating the heart is not going to provide an adequate remedy for the symptomatic dysfunction or action associated with the brain.

The brain controls all other aspects of the body. The heart sends and pumps blood through the system. Now replace the term blood for money. In terms of the other vital parts of the body, think in terms of cling-ons, moneylenders, mortgage brokers, accountants, and those who direct people to a lending authority or the source of money supply—our life blood—in essence controlling us via the heart.

If the Australian police have already declared that they are unable to control the drug market in Australia, how then can they control the financial market with overseas ownership for a large part of the Australian banking and financial system? Furthermore, is what they are doing illegal? Let us not confuse immorality with illegality. Australia is just one country. If you look at the international scenario, do they not control the finance sectors internationally? Who are these controllers? Some have indicated the Illuminati, the Rothschilds, and other famous people. Are they responsible? I think not.

You, as a customer, default on your commitments. This causes the banks to protect their interests and place you in a state of delinquency. If you cannot meet your commitments and default, the bank must protect their interests to cover their exposure. This is simply normal operating procedure. This is life.

This is the perception portrayed. You and I are totally unaware that this system exists, is being used, and is designed to assist some to default when the established parameters are identified.

People within the system have someone positioned to acquire your assets at a price below market value. You suffer a loss of self-respect for allowing this situation to come about. You are experiencing emotional turmoil, and you disappear to your own sanctuary of depression, doubt, and a loss of faith in your inability to cope with this situation.

We may subscribe to a common call for a royal commission into banks and how they are functioning. Should we not direct our attention to the brain, we cannot do without the banks and the banking system. Would it be more beneficial to ascertain who or what constitutes the brain that controls the function and then look at how we can correct that function? Will an investigation into the banks reveal this?

Before we do this, do we not need to correctly identify that the situations I have outlined exist? How can we do this? Create awareness. How do we achieve that? How can we clearly identify that these situations that I have outlined exist? Am I gifted with creative aspects, imagination, and delusional strengths that only I possess?

Having proven to ourselves that this situation exists and that it is having an adverse effect on large sections of our community, perhaps we can address the problem.

This would be an object lesson. What is the problem? Have we accepted this as a problem that exists? Do we need to establish that a problem exists, identify what the problem is, and determine the symptoms?

To achieve this, we need to correctly identify the brain or controller and establish all the controlling systems or elements that are part and parcel of the system—the legs, the arms, the eyes, the nervous, and associated systems. Again, replace this terminology with the banks, bank staff, mortgage brokers, financial consultants, feeders, and cling-ons, and we would have a better understanding of the system.

Accept that we are prone to the same wants, needs, weaknesses, fears, and doubts as some of the staff within these areas. Ask yourself how you would react if you were positioned to earn some extra money for providing information to an individual who approached you. How would you react if your family's safety was threatened in a very subtle manner, as if some harm might come to them if you did not comply with the wishes of the parties asking you for assistance? Would you risk the safety of your family?

Listen to the news today and read what is listed in the newspapers. Are we, as a public, being guided along a path that enables the system to benefit both ways? Simply put, if you want to finance an asset, home business, or similar, the bank will lend you the money. You will pay interest on that loan, and therefore the bank makes money—again, a common business practice.

It may be private money that the bank has deposited with them, and so part of what they earn is paid out to the owner. If a mortgage broker is used, he is paid a commission both on the front end and for the period of the loan.

If you are a delinquent, you default, and the bank is forced to repossess and sell your asset to a buyer.

You have lost your asset. You're an absolute clot. How did you let yourself get into this position whereby you still owe the bank money? To recover this, they will have to pursue you endlessly.

This is a classic situation that we see every day. Ask yourself who is the villain: the bank, which is designated as the heart, or the brain as the controllers of the system? Are the banks the heart or the brain? Have you been manoeuvred into a situation? My research tells me many of you have been, as I was. Is it my imagination? Was I being delusional? If so, why was I threatened and harassed?

CHAPTER 48

had been threatened by Theo. I was sitting across the desk from Theo in his office, and as such there were no witnesses to this conversation—or for that matter, to this meeting ever having taken place. But the meeting was no figment of my imagination, and neither could it be put down in any way as an illusion or delusion. But it did convince me that the funnies that had started initially and continued when I moved interstate were not a delusion.

Subsequent events alerted me that I was under observation, because I was advised that I would be by Theo.

I had no idea of the who, why, and how, or a myriad of other possibilities that caused Theo to adopt his stance and cause the warning to be given to me. My only knowledge of Theo at that time was that he was a very successful businessman. The only action Theo warned me against continuing was my activity with an organisation called Children of Divorce. At that time, this was directed at the legal profession because they were seen to be in control of the whole structure. I had stopped all activity in relation to this, had got married again, and attempted to get on with my life.

This did not stop the harassment. Theo had passed away many years go. Based on my experiences and the events that transpired, I identified Theo was the man. If one looked at the situation, I was perceived as a threat. My actions obviously created FUD in Theo's mind. This was the trigger for the harassment.

If I knew the reason for the threat and couldn't even prove that the threat had been made, then I could not understand why I was still under surveillance and labelled as a whistle-blower. The harassment continuing.

At that time, the only other possible explanation was that there could have been some connection between Theo and my ex-wife or another relative. This was a definite possibility because my ex-wife did work for a European with the same nationality as Theo. As such, was there a connection, or was I clutching at straws?

I identified that Theo could easily be identified as one of the brains; he certainly possessed all the attributes.

I could only wonder at the continuation of the activity and by whom. His family? I had long since been inactive. It was now purely a theoretical function to protect myself.

I also had to consider who else could be a part, as well the role—a cling-on or the brain. To the list, I added Stephan. My investigations revealed he had claimed my father's superannuation entitlements and used them to satisfy his own requirements.

His activities at the time of my father's death and shortly thereafter, as well as his blocking my attempts to investigate further regaining my father's entitlements, placed him as a strong suspect in this environment. Was he working with the organisation, or was he on his own?

This relative did have some financial concerns in his business, together with the inexplicable happenings to my father at that time, causing me to become very suspicious of Stephan and his family. He and his son could be regarded as cling-ons of the system. Both were involved as mortgage brokers within the financial lending structure.

There was one other person whom I suspected. It was not too remote a connection, and in this case he was using the system to force me into a situation whereby he could relieve me of my assets. This suspect was within my family circle.

His behavioural characteristics and the way he operated and conducted himself in family gatherings alerted me as to what he was capable of. He screamed incongruence. I never dismissed the possibility of his operating with the European people whom I considered to be the number one suspect and a cancerous growth.

When considering these people, that I thought could be causing me grief, I always had to come back to what I considered to be the number one suspect that had threatened my life. From my investigations, I positioned the other suspects as cling-ons. I did not see any evidence to elevate them to the position of a brain.

However, I did believe that there could be a connection with the various people within my family circle who had been coerced to working for the cling-ons due to a threat or for a consideration, so that they could protect their interests.

CHAPTER 49

I f my theories and suppositions were correct, and the brain or brains were controlling the banks, then I had to revisit information I been given on the banking structure in Australia and overseas.

The police had firmly established that the drug business in Australia was beyond their control. This tended to agree with the previous article I had discovered that stated the banks were merely a tool and were now working in conjunction with the drug lords.

I had to consider that if the drug lords had organised the banks and big business into that form of revenue stream, it would be one short step to coerce businesses into the asset acquisition situation that I had been told was generating billions of dollars in revenue.

Supply of real estate assets in Australia and other overseas countries was unable to keep up with the demand being generated by overseas buyers. Banks, together with their connections, would be the perfect vehicle to increase supply.

I had been concentrating on the acquisition of assets, as well as the methodologies used to convert them into a sound financial structure.

Suppose that it wasn't just drug barons and drug lords using the banks as a vehicle to launder money. Look at the possibility of similar methodologies being used to create revenue that could be sent overseas.

This could be a possible revenue stream for Lebanese businessman and other involved countries to send funds back to these countries. The funds were essential for them to continue their fight against the forces that they wished to dispose of. This method of revenue generation lends itself to being employed in a variety of areas for many reasons. Some of the Moslem people could be using this methodology to help their fellow countrymen in their home country. It could also be used to further develop and fund their beliefs in Australia and other Western countries.

As I have established and identified by the police, where do you draw the line between generating income (using drugs as the source to satisfy this objective, an ego state, or the drive for possession) and generating revenue for two ulterior purposes in other countries?

After examining the banking structure in Australia and the ownership of banks with their American interests, is it possible that once more we are exposed to the controlling aspects of individuals and their grab for power? Furthermore, this appears to be operating on an international level.

We have been told by several people that there are an elite few who wish to acquire a position of world dominance. These people are said to have financed the world wars for both sides and are at the centre of returning world dominance and power. One of the theories is that it is their intent to reduce the world population to more manageable levels because our current growth situation is taking us beyond levels that we can sustain.

My starting on this discovery trail after the initial threat was caused by fear of what I was supposed to know about their operation. I had further verification that there are many systems in place, with one at the expense of a large section of the general population.

The operational finesse of this situation was increasingly made clear to me by my European contact as to how the mechanism worked and the methodologies used to assist.

I could observe the role and the methodology used by staff, primarily in the loan department of the bank and supported by senior staff to achieve their desired objectives. It was during this period that I identified the banks as the heart of the operation. Without this lifeblood within the heart, the entire mechanism, and our society, would grind to a halt in so many ways.

I also determined that the banks are also a victim of the system as much as you and me.

If we accept that these situations are happening to us in everyday life and that in many aspects we are being controlled by the gifted few, we must accept that this situation is not an original situation. From my investigation, this situation embraces all levels of society in a variety of areas, especially those we deemed as the pillars of our society: judges, solicitors, accountants, and financial advisors form part of the operational expertise within the system. Again, it would be unjust to label all the people as being active operational members in the system.

Just as we can't embrace all the people within the professional areas of our industries, it would be unjust to blame all the people within the banking sector. As we have seen, some of them have made information public to their own detriment.

You then have a choice to make. Do you believe that the situation outlined by me exists, and that many people are losing their possessions and their assets? In the case of the divorce, their children are disadvantaged, and because of this, the public are being financially and psychologically handicapped in many different ways. Do we believe that these people wouldn't do this to us?

Alternatively, do we believe that I was not threatened by Theo, that I was not told I would be found in the back of a burnt-out car, that I was not told I would be sent back to my wife with my face rearranged, that I did not have the names of the banking staff removed from my computer, and that I did not experience the continuing factors employed by the bank when I was going through my building project?

Was this coincidence? Was I being delusional? As I had been told many times, this was a mistake on my behalf and a figment of my imagination. I have no evidence or proof, do I?

I had long ago established that I had no evidence to prove my belief, and that I had seen and heard many things in the media confirming my belief and my experience. My belief is that the proof is out there with the public. They are being subjected to the system, and in most cases they are unaware of the system. They believe that the banks are the main offenders, and they want enquiries into the banking system. Have I just stumbled into a system run locally by the cling-ons?

One would not expect the pillars of our society to be involved in something such as this, would we? We cannot accept that this type of situation, as depicted by me, could be allowed to continue, particularly when we consider that there are many people within these sectors who have confirmed my theories.

Can we accept that this is prevalent and has been for a long time? What lets these people who are aware of the situation allow it to continue? Is it fear, financial gain, and ego?

But really, it is all a case of my vivid imagination, and I'm being delusional, aren't I? This type of thing couldn't happen. Could it?

Whatever you believe, look out there and ask, "Could this all be true?" It is fiction, isn't it? This can't be true, can it? Can it?

History tells us that countries were overrun by marauding tribes—the Spaniards, the Romans, and the Greeks, to name but a few. Rape and pillage was standard fare. Are the same processes in place today but with different methodologies?

I am one individual accused of paranoia, a vivid imagination, and fantasy. They say I'm totally incapable of doing anything constructive to end this situation. I was persuaded to not continue. A situation like this cannot be attempted by one person. You are the judge—form your own opinions and do your own homework. Talk to your friends who have been placed in the situations either through divorce, life, or business situations. They have lost their possessions, been made bankrupt and watched the dissolution of their lives. Talk to the Children of Divorce members.

First, you must decide whether what I have outlined is fact or fiction. I have spent a lifetime trying to do just that. Have you or your friends been a victim of the system? Then ask yourself, "Can we escape from the system? How?" The police have given up on drugs. Is this another area that we must give up on and submit to? Remember that every day, children are being affected by broken families, destitute parents, and situations that they have been placed into so that the controllers, organisers, and cling-ons can make money.

You are the judge. I have identified some of the potential victims and the supply lines. I have identified the heart of the situation. The brains are clouded in mystery, seeking world dominance fulfilling their egos. They influence and control our lives and, most important, our children's lives.

How do we stop them and start taking our lives back from the Shouldabaters, Mustabaters, cling-ons, and controllers? We must use our own unique qualities that we possess, given to us by the guy with the long flowing gown, the beard, and the shepherd's crook. Call it universal law or whatever you believe in.

In terms of those much more learned than I, how do we escape the system? Together, can we start to take our lives back? Can we?

Printed in the United States
By Bookmasters